THE ARISTOCRAT

Other titles in the
Extraordinary Classics series

Daniil Kharms
Incidences

Olive Moore
Fugue

Juan Carlos Onetti
A Brief Life
The Shipyard

Fernando Pessoa
The Book of Disquiet

Robert Walser
The Walk

Ernst Weiss

THE ARISTOCRAT

Boëtius von Orlamünde

*Translated, with an afterword,
by Martin Chalmers*

An Extraordinary Classic

Series Editors: Pete Ayrton and Martin Chalmers

Library of Congress Catalog Card Number: 94–67450

A complete catalogue record for this book can be obtained from the British Library on request

First published as *Boëtius von Orlamünde* in 1928 by S Fischer Verlag, Berlin
Published as *Der Aristokrat* in 1930 by S Fischer Verlag, Berlin

This edition first published in 1994 by
Serpent's Tail, 4 Blackstock Mews, London N4, and 401 West Broadway #1, New York, NY 10012

Phototypeset in 10/13 pt Galliard by Intype, London
Printed in Finland by Werner Söderström Oy

This translation is published with the help of Inter Naciones, Bonn

THE ARISTOCRAT

PART ONE

1

My name is Boëtius Maria Dagobert von Orlamünde, or rather I call myself Orlamünde. The historical family of Orlamünde died out in the sixteenth century. So Orlamünde is merely a name here. I am descended from another ancient noble family, which I do not wish to mention. Despite my high-sounding name I am worth little. My parents also lived in the most wretched circumstances. Did they know it? Did they deceive themselves? They still possessed vestiges of earlier splendour, but they went hungry, and our old servant David with them. Instead, however, of discarding their noble status and taking up a bourgeois profession and in this way drawing the most obvious conclusion from the decline of the once mighty Lords of Orlamünde, they bestowed upon me, their only child, besides the gifts of poverty and frugality, the truly absurd Christian name of Boëtius as well. That was far from all. In their blindness they believed it necessary to give me a "princely" education. First I am educated at home by an old abbé, later my beloved father puts me in a noble boys' college, if I may call it that, an extensive establishment at which the offspring of the houses of pure blood, whom for some reason one will not or cannot educate at home, receive an education in accordance with their rank. This noble boys' college is called Onderkuhle and is situated in eastern Belgium, not far from the frontier.

In my first year I disappear among these young lords as the boy who is at once the smallest, the poorest, the most timid and the most red-haired. Red-haired – as clear as the words are and as precisely as they characterise a man externally – is not quite the right expression. It is true that I have the pale blue, watery eyes of most red-haired people. Certainly I have their buttercream complexion, sprinkled with reddish brown freckles, the long delicate hands, the angular yet inwardly somehow crooked figure and boneless form, such as many very blond or red-haired youths have, and it is this physical disposition which makes me incapable of elegant dance, of any proper bow, of any "noble bearing". One only has to see with what indescribable clumsiness, stiffness and awkwardness, to the astonishment of the Master of Ceremonies, I receive on my great day my final report from the somewhat trembling, red and puffy hand of the old Headmaster of Onderkuhle; so as not to put me to shame, he looks away with his likewise trembling and slightly glazed eyes, whereas precisely his gaze fixed firmly upon me would have had the power to restore my self-confidence, my healthy, manly posture, my trust in myself and in a world which is, for all its terrors, nevertheless benevolent. No, he looks away, into the corner where the old blue school flags hang. Why a school should own flags has never been clear to me. After all, it neither marches into battle, nor does it number veterans, wounded and D. in its ranks. But the flags are there and the pride of all. The Steward, Master of Ceremonies and teacher of etiquette in one (his name is Garnier), he, who is said to be the child of a Russian bondsman and a French chambermaid and who, despite his apparently quite subordinate rank, commands the whole army of orderlies, servants and functionaries, this man cleans them every morning, before he begins his inspection of the establishment and of our estate. And he does this by rubbing the black flagstaffs with a white silk cloth, and then running his thumb over the old gilded hexagonal shields, which are fixed to the flagstaffs with golden nails. The flags themselves he does not clean, because they must look as old and venerable as possible. He must not use a brush, he merely rearranges the folds and lets the blue fringes run through his old "princely", beautiful, ivory coloured, ring adorned fingers.

What are these flags doing in the noble school? What of the alcoholic Headmaster's unsteady gaze, this old gentleman in his buttoned up uniform, which resembles that of a cavalry colonel, but bears even more gold embroidered on it? What am I doing, standing on a platform, no, in front of it, on the shiny smooth parquet floor? I place my right foot on the podium and in this most ridiculous position in the world receive my report from the hand of the school's senior master who stubbornly looks away. How lacking it all is in reason! Admittedly it is beautiful and arouses nobler feelings in some. Furthermore, this scene does not take place in Germany, Austria or Sweden, the three most rational countries in Europe, but in Catholic Belgium, where appearance is also given its due. And indeed appearance is everything. I, the aristocrat of ancient family and a beggar, my marks, which demonstrate nothing worthy of a mark (for skill in riding, fencing, swimming, gymnastics are not proven by stamped certificates), the Headmaster, who has never smelt powder, in his colonel's uniform, the flags, which one is not allowed to dust, the Steward, who is the real master of the school, for he, like so many servants in the world, rules over those who believe they possess power, but who lack the courage to make use of it.

In the school at Onderkuhle (in our country its fame is so great that one only needs to say, I was educated at Onderkuhle . . .) my dear teachers taught me to ride excellently. There were two riding teachers, one was a graduate of the cavalry course in Brussels, the other a former champion amateur horseman; both were altogether satisfied with me. In riding and fencing my fairly casual posture (people sometimes call it gawky) has probably been of considerable use to me. This posture only looks clumsy, but is by no means so, especially not on the back of a horse. In riding one must not forget that one living body is moving in a degree of harmony with another. The more easily the displacement of weight takes place and the more the rider adapts to the horse, both in his muscle control while sitting in the saddle and in the distribution of weight, in the course of which one must often allow one's feeling to play as if with a pair of goldsmith's scales, the more harmonious are the fundamentally firm paces that result. May I express it quite plainly: when a competent rider sits on a good horse, the rider no more commands the horse than the horse commands him. Both are indissolubly united, one flesh and, for the duration of the riding lesson at least, also one soul.

Now I cannot expect, that from my confused attempt to portray it, the reader has by this point already formed a picture of how I live and how I pass my childhood from my tenth year on. Result: I can ride and drive a carriage, swim, fence, fire pistols, know the principal features of the drill book in their practical application, the basic facts of geography and history are familiar to me. No sport is an effort for me, each one gives me pleasure, but I cannot count properly, nor write quite without errors.

Not without cause did our Master of Ceremonies – whom I earlier described as the issue of a voluntary bondsman and of a French maid – take first place beside our spiritual shepherd. Exercising under the command of a tutor lasts only half an hour each day. Admittedly the Abbé, a very important person in our little state, supervises our conscience, prescribes the usual, for a Catholic believer, easy exercises and prayers and attaches great importance to regular confession and to our diligence in the religious instruction class. The whole day long, however, from early morning till late evening, we are subject to the gaze of the Master, who has to teach us "the forms". Above all the greeting. All have to file past his person. We are bare-headed. On his coal black hair, which, however, is already flecked with grey at the temples, he is wearing a cap. We must come to a halt three paces from him. "Back, back!" he shouts at us, as if he were afraid we wanted to throw ourselves on him. Now he looks at us with his Slav eyes, so that we make a deep bow. Never deep enough. No royal highness has received so many bows from high aristocrats as he. He plays the ruler for so long, until we see the ruler in him. Answering, remaining silent, allowing precedence, taking precedence, etiquette at table, greeting and leavetaking of those of higher rank, of equal rank, domestics, all refinements of aristocratic intercourse, deportment, spiritual disposition, self-control, tact, ease in giving commands and above all constantly keeping distance and remaining conscious of one's situation – these are the subjects which he teaches. Hour after hour, at meal times, even when we are sleeping. His slate grey, rather wide set eyes are everywhere. We shall never become masters in his lessons. He acts as if he had grown up with it, and yet it is well known that he spent only one year with Count F. in St Petersburg. The latter, admittedly was the most complete courtier of his time.

To fence well with the foil (an art in which my apparently

boneless body renders me most excellent service), is more important, he says, than accumulation of dead knowledge and counting with decimal fractions. For religion the young aristocrat had his father confessor, for politics his king, for the administration of property and finances his bookkeeper. Fundamentally decimal fractions did not exist at all, and even if they did exist, it did not become a man of good family to oversee his servants with regard to such trifles.

That is the character of our education. The Headmaster is a gold-embroidered shadow. The Abbé is always in the beyond, but the Master rules here. My father lives far away.

I could train as a jockey, as a fencing master, so great is my experience. My wrist and my spine (the latter is of the greatest importance) never lose their suppleness. But fencing teacher! What a fanciful profession in an age which no longer knows the duel, the decisive single combat, God's judgement at the tip of the rapier. And jockey? No. The real, the bloody fencing hall of the age now lies elsewhere.

Thus I live in the exclusive college until my eighteenth year; highly respected by all as good horsemen and fencer, even by the morose Russian Master of Ceremonies. If I have no money (one needs money everywhere, even here), then no one mentions it, provided only that otherwise I do my name credit – and at least I do not discredit it.

A happy childhood? I cannot complain.

2

I still remember one day, a drive in the wood. A small stud-farm also belonged to the college. We had more than enough free horses, not all could be used as farm and school horses. The model estate that was attached to the school in Onder-kuhle did not yet need all the draught animals, it was before the harvest, the beginning of July perhaps. I was deputising for one of the riding teachers, who was away (when a teacher was sick, he was said to be away), and this honorary office gave me many advantages. I was at this time older than most of the other pupils, was not assigned to any class (of which there were five) and every day expected that it would be suggested to me that I take up a profession and leave Ond-erkuhle.

The day was all the more beautiful. The stable-boys pulled our honey coloured gig out of the shed, it was a high, two wheeled well sprung trap. We, my friend Titurel and I, harnessed a young little horse, not yet three years old, whose delicate, very yielding body did not entirely fill out the girths and bands, but moved in them like a man in a suit that is too large; likewise at home our old servant David shrank from year to year inside his violet-ink coloured livery, his coat hung down to his knee and later even further. With him it was old age and end, with our little horse youth and beginning. Now the little horse set off, constantly and unthinkingly turning his head to look at us, sitting back to back in the gig, and opening his gleaming mouth to whinny. Since he is inconvenienced by the traces and the bit, the animal rolls out his broad black lips, which are bright red on the inside, giving the head, which remains shaggy despite all the brushing, a comical, boyish, jolly appearance. So the horse trots with us through the park to a nearby lake, which is no longer part of our estate. Do I not say *our* estate, as if all of it, stables, farm buildings, accounts office, labourers' quarters, wells and horse-ponds, fire-house, granaries, byres, pigsties, dovecots and the fenced-in space with guinea fowl, peacocks, turkeys, the shed with the ploughs, with the steam threshing machine and the mechanical tedder were my personal property? And yet I own nothing. Not even the whip, which I calmly hold in my hand, without even touching the delicate, trembling skin of the fallow dun with the tip.

We go past the dung-pits at a fast trot, and follow a narrow track into the orchards, where all the blossom has already faded. Yet remnants of white feathery blossom have been left behind on the ground about the black trunks of the apple trees, which are gleaming brightly in the sun, as if varnished. The day is cloudless. No wind. At night only a little dew beneath the magnificent shining moon; we are not wearing any uniform cap (we were all in a kind of uniform, I already mentioned those of the Headmaster and of the school teachers' servant). Only I do not like to remove the cap, for good reason; but now I hold it between my knees. It crunches when the carriage pitches and sways. Gloves are nevertheless put on, as that is the rule and the Master has his eyes everywhere. Now, however, as we leave the boundary of the estate behind, I pull the gloves off, and while the fragile conveyance rocks back and forward at my movement, I tuck the gloves, folded together, the inside facing out, into my friend's breast pocket.

At the bend in the track one catches sight through the bushes of the school building, like a castle built of red brick, the further away one goes, the larger and mightier it seems to become and the higher it seems to soar up from the quite insignificant hill into the clear, shimmering summer afternoon air. Now at a sharp turning in the way it lies behind us, we drive on beneath young lime trees, then the track bends to join an avenue of poplars (called the Italian Avenue), beyond which on both sides there is a fir wood. There is silence, only a cuckoo calls quite far away. The carriage moves so lightly and so fast, the horse steps so regularly and firmly in its too loose harness, that we seem to glide along under the tall malachite green firs as if on rails. To the fragrance of the trees is added the smell of cart-grease, which drips so copiously from the wheel hubs that the bushes, rowans, sorrel ferns, broom and the tall grey-green docks, shooting up to a giant size in the damp earth, are spattered by it. I glance round and observe my friend engaged in drawing the glove, which I had given him for safekeeping, from his pocket, turning it round and raising it to his bare, cropped head, and pressing it against his freckled cheeks, perhaps to test the softness of the leather. But there is not much sense in that; for since the pupils' parents have to supply gloves and caps, though nothing else besides, gloves are for me a very precious, much husbanded article. I know that my father cannot send me more than two or three pairs every year.

I have not yet spoken a single word of him, my Master, my old Master, of whom my heart is even now thinking. I want to see only the earthy, chocolate coloured woodland floor in front of me, smelling cleanly of firs and broom as it unrolls beneath the shiny, polished, sparkling black hooves of the little horse. We're going uphill, towards the little lake. Here stand beech trees and oaks. Amid the bright downy foliage the serious ore-like green of the conifers is sprouting, among which the pale green young shoots on the twigs shine like fruit with an almost dazzling brilliance. A sky of noble blue rises above the entwined crowns of the trees gently trembling in the summer evening wind. Then the track opens out, the outflow of the deep blue lake rushes with a muted swirl over a smoothly polished weir made of white tree trunks to which fluttering algae thin as hair and strips of dark brown fleshy moss have attached themselves. So the completely clear water pours away in two tones, in alternating stripes. There is one other object on earth which is similarly striped or checked, if not in such beautiful colours – I say it at last, it is the hair on my head, which through a strange trick of nature has two colours at once, one more yellowish (at the temples), the other more reddish (on the crown). Not everyone notices, perhaps only someone who knows. Perhaps I alone see myself so. As long as I can conceal it, as now beneath the pike coloured uniform cap, which I have put on as if I was shivering in the cooler breath of the water, then I am at ease. But how will things turn out once I have to give up the pale grey cap, return the likewise pike coloured uniform to the Russian bondsman, the master of the house, in order then to step out into life, of whose cruelty my poor father has told me so much, when he visits me here, in all my red-haired ugliness, without knowledge and useful skills?

He is called the Prince, and princely he was from birth, his bearing is without blemish, his disposition noble, his words are well chosen, his dress is of the most unassuming elegance, on leavetaking he gives the servants the largest tips, presents a golden needle with a horseshoe to the orderly who has tidied his room and dusted his shining patent leather shoes. He gives with both hands, he makes presents almost heedlessly, heedless with joy at living here with his son. So, with his nobleman's gait, a calm sovereign power in his slate grey eyes, he makes an appearance in all the old brilliance, like a rich man, like the owner of a great feudal estate, or like a prince of royal blood, who as a cavalry general on a tour of inspection only travels in a special train and never without his adjutants and two valets. If, however, my father has found a moment to be alone with me, how many melancholy things must I hear, how anxious do I become, how humbly do I listen to his refined precepts, which, however, he himself in truth knows cannot be followed. We walk past the school chapel and watch the farmyard birds disporting themselves on the steps. The words "hardships" and "in accordance with one's rank" occur most frequently. We talk unceasingly of the future, without leaving the vicinity of the little place of worship. But what "future" means for me, never becomes quite clear. A life pension, which is not, however, sufficient to live on, only for doing without, is granted my parents by very wealthy relations in Ireland whom no one has ever met. A string of pearls, a combination of both reddish and black gems, the last remnant of a priceless family hierloom, has been pledged or is to be so – yet this is not easily accomplished in secret, and the world, the public should only know *that* we live, but not *how*. Here his countenance becomes very serious, his long, gloved hands reach first for my arm, then for my head, he pulls off my cap and looks at it. He too, twenty and more years ago, wore a similar one, happy, aristocratic and carefree – and since he does not wish to cloud my happy, carefree youth, he suddenly falls silent and gives the cap back to me. If he knew how much D. exercises me at this moment – he would speak differently. But he acts as if everything were easy for him, as if he would smile at everything. He opens wide his slate coloured eyes, in which the bright steps of the little chapel with the even smaller hens are reflected in miniature, and now he moistens his thick, somewhat drooping, lips with his tongue. Does he know nothing? Does he not know me? Not know himself? Or is it embarrassment and shame?

3

It is now six months since the last time my old father was here, I remember precisely, because it was his last visit. But now I do not want to speak of the "last", not of D., however profoundly both are related, not of old, even if he, my dearest father, was then as old as I, thanks to a beautiful D., hope never to be.

The bridge over the outflow of the lake, across which our little carriage is rocking now, is not so new either. The wood is soft and rotten, it smells of the fungi which flourish in considerable quantity underneath the little bridge and there undermine the decaying woodwork. I drive more slowly, not out of fear that the bridge could give way under our weight, but so that my young horse does not catch its narrow hooves between the wooden beams and stumble.

Strangers pass us, the women wear large greenish-white coifs coming down past their eyes, whose gleam nevertheless twinkles through the holes in the embroidery. The men march in high boots, long beards around their mouths. If one now remembers school lessons amongst the chattering, usually good-natured but often also malicious comrades in Onderkuhle and if one now sees the bridge, the lake before one instead of the familiar institution walls, then one glimpses at this moment a long and varied, inexhaustible life before one. Everything is full of hope.

My friend Titurel, who has not yet quite recovered from his last illness (he always finds it so hard to be done with things, including his exercises), owes this afternoon's holiday and the permission for the drive to just this weakness and the need for recovery. As we now leave the lake behind us and at a faster pace proceed along the highway towards the town between fields of potato and beet and well watered meadows, his back presses more firmly against me. The gig pitches. Something or other in the spring mechanism has clicked suspiciously. I brake and bring the horse to a stop, and not by pulling at the reins, but more by slackening them. I begin to whistle very softly as well, a command which my little horse understands immediately and obeys. I trained him in his time, with a soft coaxing hand taught him the first proper paces at the lunge and accustomed him to the completely unfamiliar bit, which at first was incomprehensible to him.

My friend now slides down from his seat with great rapidity, without reflecting that he thereby pulls up the front of the shaft and does not exactly do the animal's mouth, which is still very soft, any good; now he stands before me and wants to help me down from my seat. I look around, in case there is another carriage or an automobile coming down the road. Suddenly I feel the ankle of my left foot grasped by Titurel's hand. He holds something soft under my foot, on which I am about to jump down as gently as possible so as not to jerk the fragile carriage too greatly. Now I stand on the ground, in front of me my friend, who has offered me his left hand with my gloves as footrest. Did he wish to render me an especially chivalrous service, as is indicated by a crooked smile on his closed lips? His teeth are bad, out of shame he opens his mouth as little as possible. Consequently he often appears shy, which he is not, ironic rather. But I gave him the gloves for safekeeping, not for chivalrous services. I now see before me my old father, thought of whom I have until now forcibly repressed. I know how difficult it will be for him to afford the money for a new pair. His own, after all, he wears only on "parade", that is on visits to Onderkuhle or for important events and state visits at which his presence, that is, his name, is expected. My friend is silent. Presumably he awaits a cordial word from me. I cannot, however control my anger. Without speaking, I take the damp, soiled gloves out of his hand and throw them, as if they had now become quite worthless, over my shoulders into the beet fields behind me. Then I bend down under the carriage and discover that a regulator screw on the right spring shackle-strap has loosened. I can grip and tighten it with the use of one of my keys.

Then we mount and return the same way. Yet it is not the same any more. On the forest track we hear a carriage coming up behind us. Our backs have already separated long ago. We sit there stiff and to attention, no one, not even the Master of Ceremonies, could find any fault. Bearing is all that he knows, never heart, never feeling. Does he not know D. either? Does he know it? I urge my horse on, I do not spare the whip. Nevertheless the other carriage overtakes us. In it sits the Master of Ceremonies, who does not seem to recognise us. He neither expects a greeting, nor does he think of returning ours. Perhaps at this unofficial moment he is not thinking of us, the pupils, but of himself and his "private" riches, which he is said to have accumulated here and which will soon also allow him an estate away from Onderkuhle. Whom will he command in Brussels? With heavy lowered eyes, he leans back proud and alone in his carriage. The horses whinny to one another, his also are not old, pure blooded and not yet long together as a team. Now and again the shadow of the trees plays on their lean haunches, on the smooth surfaces of the broad cruppers, shining like ripe chestnuts, and on the sharply angled sides of the neck under the very close trimmed mane. A gentle wind has risen. The light of the setting sun is occasionally obscured. Rain is in the air with the red glow. The cuckoo can no longer be heard. The bridge is very dark and now smells even more strongly of mould and decay. The Bondsman's horses turn their heads towards us. In the big swamp brown eyes of one, I see reflected the lake or the foliage, half blue, half green, only an illusion, only a moment, a gleam. My horse begins to sweat, and the skin darkens first at the edges of the harness, then the little hairs stick together, stand up in rows, as if they had been groomed with a wide-toothed comb. Now there's a smell, heavy and aromatic, of sweat, of firs, rain and dust.

It was early evening, the boys of the "Fifth" were on the tennis courts, where the balls flew through the twilight, pale against the dark wire nets. Then comes the thud of the balls against the tightly stretched strings of the rackets and the even keeping of the score, in which I recognise the rather plummy voice of young Prince X. (Piggy), who likes to assume this office, but does not like to enter a contest. But when it comes to giving a sleeping pupil a "dousing" at night with a watering can, then he's first to join in. He knows about "flea powder" too and the "Russian lesson". But he himself is always "neutral".

The younger boys are playing croquet on a lawn nearby. Their yelling and laughter is very loud, it often drowns out the mallet blows. From time to time one of them also cries out, when a fellow pupil, whether through clumsiness (as he says) or out of malice (as it usually is) or "to put the man to the test", has struck him on the heel or the knee cap with the mallet. I too know this pain. During my first years here I was spared none of these merciless tests which are nevertheless essential for achieving the rank of "man". At home no one punished me. I did not know what physical pain is. Neither did I consider it to be a punishment here, unlike Prince X. I never complained to the teachers or to the Master of Ceremonies about an older and stronger fellow pupil, although at night I often could not sleep with the pain. For there were many tests.

Now the teachers in their light, white undress jackets are resting on the garden chairs, which are covered in red and white striped linen, the clouds from their cigars gather into a blue diadem beneath the tall summer trees. The Russian is already walking back and forward between them and the playing fields, ostensibly to enquire about the teachers' wishes, in reality to keep an eye on everyone, teachers and pupils.

Now we are in the yard by the stables. His horses are already unharnessed. A stable boy (Fredy) rubs down their backs and stomachs with dry straw. Usually they disdain straw altogether, but now they snap at it with their long tongues, pale red like strawberry ice, and show their dark, dully gleaming, ivory coloured teeth, catching the sleeve of the anxiously laughing stable boy as they do so. My horse again opens his mouth to whinny, raising his fine triangular head a little and looking round to the stable entrance. When I look at him, he stands still again, only prancing a little on his front legs. The reins have been looped around the brake handle in a firm knot. I want to help my friend Titurel down from the seat. He is so quiet, quieter than usual. Now he falls into my arms like a lifeless mass, he looks at me with his all too shiny, yellowish eyes, wants to laugh, but only uncontrolled spasms cross his pale, freckled, rather coarse face. He does not complain. He does not show his teeth. He trembles, presumably because of a chill, and so, without any special effort, I then take him in my arms although I am smaller than he, and carry him across the yard, where he is received by the duty junior tutor, sternly reprimanded, and immediately got over to the infirmary. When I turn around, the carriage is no longer standing in front of the steps, but my little horse has freed himself from the stable lad, he trots around between the buildings, glowing in the evening sun, roguishly flicking his long tail, whinnying unceasingly, capriciously raising and lowering his voice, as if talking to himself. Now he has reached the clipped hedge, which separates the playing fields from the farm buildings, and lets himself go with joyful cries and high jumps across the dark green bushes.

Who would not change places with him? No longer to be Boëtius von Orlamünde, but a three-year-old, strong, completely healthy and beautiful animal, which knows nothing of D., which is completely absorbed by life.

I love animals greatly, but something of this love is envy.

4

I did not sleep very well during the night that followed, since I was forced to think extremely hard about my father, the creator of my life, and about Titurel, my only friend, and so it happens that in the morning, still drowsy, I stumble as I cross the threshold. This year I no longer live together with the other pupils in one of the large dormitories. There are seven of them, some have already been lying empty for a long time. The house could accommodate more pupils than were there now. The Headmaster, the Abbé and the Master only chose the "purest names" from the many nominations – often only one brother, if three had applied. Supposedly, however, many more pupils were entered in the books – to the advantage of the Master. I have never been able to discover anything certain. It also does not concern me.

Although surplus in the bookkeeping, since not assignable to any school class, I am allowed to live in Onderkuhle, as my family has not yet decided my future. I have been accommodated, for the time being it is said, in a small room, which is adjacent to the dormitory of the fifth class, a narrow, if also high and bright room, which loses much of its cosiness because a quantity of old furniture, bedside tables and tall lecterns is crowded into it. If in the evening one has brought back a few flowers from a walk, then one has to place them on the sloping top of a high desk or put them in water in an old ink well. The clothes which every pupil must brush himself, lie across a bedside table. If, as sometimes happens one is unable to sleep at night, and wants to reach for a book, one has to pick it out of the depths of a drawer, then take up position at the lectern, and so try to read like a bookkeeper at his desk, in which case the shoulders and the drooping head grow tired more quickly than the legs. The whip, which I have brought to my room, hangs sideways from the desk on a nail which is really intended for rulers. All in all my bedroom looks more like an office, and hence also my deep distaste for it, and hence also in certain connections my deep distaste for offices, counting rooms, clerical work and numbers.

Why, as one of the oldest pupils, who often deputises for the riding and fencing teachers, was I not permitted to feel myself still to be a child, at least in the evenings and at night, and to have my bed in the same row as the other pupils' beds? Does the Master want to make me like him? Am I to be a person requiring respect like him? How infinitely reassuring it would be to hear my comrades breathing beside me, when I cannot sleep. How marvellous it is to pass a last minute in bed in the mornings when the other boys are already leaving theirs and have proceeded, laughing and shouting, to the washrooms! How wonderful a cigarette tastes, when the tip, still warm from my neighbour's lips, is put between my lips at night, for the vice of smoking is rife in the senior classes at Onderkuhle, but equally also the virtue of comradeship, of sharing everything with one's peers, who together form a large united family. At night we know one another by different means, which we have drawn from our reading (we learn little, but we read much). So my friend, whom I earlier called Titurel, is only so named at night, by day he is bearer of one of the most famous names of Belgium. I am called Tyl, and since the names go together well, we are often mentioned in the same breath. Otherwise my joys are so innocent that the father confessor, who learns of them each Thursday, only imposes the most minor penance for them and trusts without further ado my promise never to commit these sins again. There is a sympathy of such purity between my comrades and myself, that when I have to deputise for a teacher, I completely forget that the boy with the blueish gleaming foil, who now "stands on guard" in front of me on the black carpet in the fencing room and feigns a naive defensive position, or the other one, who stands beside the harnessed but stirrupless and unsaddled horse and waits for a sign from me to mount – yes, I forget completely that I know this boy, that at night I have slept near him, that I know the taste of his lips and that I have smoked cigarettes still warm from his mouth. By day I know of no Titurel, I am no longer Tyl, I do my duty. I could still easily have been allowed a place among the younger boys this year. The old Bondsman, the Master, however, did not wish it. Everything submits to him, and yet his gaze is not steady, his blood is not noble, his hands are not clean either, I know everything about him, he nothing about me.

I told of the night, of my sleeping badly. It is not the dreams of youth, sick with longing, which wake me, which make me press my ear against the door of the neighbouring dormitory, from which sounds the gentle, drawn out breathing of the "Fifth", not with youth's hunger for love do I try to catch their all too quiet conversations, not out of desire for cigarettes or tobacco, to draw in the cigarette smoke, which seeps through the joints, does my open mouth nestle up against the cracks in the door – what excites me is something quiet different. Something else makes me get up and, my shoulders hunched, press myself first against one then against the other useless, tall lectern. It is a feeling that one will not suspect in a seventeen year old. But will one believe that this feeling, which I must name only too soon, has been active in my soul since it was a soul, for as long as I can remember at all? I must name it – but I am afraid even of the words. It is fear of death.

The next morning I leave my room after I have, clumsily enough, washed myself at one of the desks, which has been transformed into a wash stand and after I have again concealed the last letter from my father, already several months old, in the drawer of the bedside table – for there is no other table in this room, no cupboard either, such as the other pupils have – then I step out and on the threshold stumble over a soft but sinewy object. I lift it up, perhaps it is a sandwich wrapped in silk paper, which one of the boys has lost, although I would not know either how – but it is my gloves, which yesterday, during the drive, I threw into a beet field. They are cleaned, even if not completely; are dry; the earth has been removed from the seams, they are serviceable, even if one cannot do oneself any particular credit with them. A service has been rendered to me by their return, I cannot deny it, and I am happy to have them again. But has my Titurel not been taken to the infirmary seriously ill? Was watch not kept at his bed? If he was indeed so foolish, so feverishly and boyishly headstrong, why was he not prevented from leaving his bed, from covering the whole of the long track past the lake during the rainy night? I know the rain poured from the sky, because during the night I had several times put my head out of the window. It made me,

the healthy one, shiver, but he had so far overcome fear
of the consequences, the dread of D., that out of a spirit of
chivalry, in this a true Titurel, he set out on the long road,
dragged himself through the beet fields, until he found the
gloves again. I can see that they are mine, the initials B. v.
O. are marked on the inside in faded violet-reddish ink.
Although I have washed the pair of gloves often enough
with Venice-soap, these marks will never quite be obliterated.
I no longer remember when they were inscribed.

But they remain inscribed like the feeling of death in my
soul. Now one knows what it is.

5

_____

A life that is unceasingly in the power of D., is as good as no life at all. One wants to liberate oneself from it. One wants to forget D., wants to work, one must work after all, since life makes demands, to which all submit, even the Orlamündes. If one is successful, one can provide for oneself, for others. One has friends, who are close, who breathe not far away, in their high, spacious bedchambers, one has parents, of whom one can think only with longing, sympathy and with an almost indescribable feeling: this feeling is similar to that which someone has when, in winter, he returns home in the late evening and undresses in comfort before going to bed, and then, suffused with just this indescribable feeling, leans with his back against the warm stove in the room which has been darkened again. The warmth rises almost magically up to the bare neck beside the wide collar of the night shirt. Now one has a sense of the length, of the boundlessness of existence. That is more wonderful than everything else. One breathes so softly, that it is as if one were not breathing. And if the stove now flares up and radiates stronger heat, it is as if it is wrapping the boy standing against it from feet to neck in heavy blankets still warm from the horse's body.

So it would be for me, if I were allowed always to live

with my parents, if I were allowed to eat at the same table, if I were allowed to go out riding beside my father in the big public park in Brussels. Our horses would be in step, their heads nod in time, the girths and bands creak. Fine brown dust rises from the bark which covers the paths, as if moles were pushing their heads up from below. The rather pale, drooping lips of the Master (let me call my father the Master, I would so like to see him as great; to know myself small beside him makes me feel happy), the Master's pale reddish lips moisten, since in the rare pleasure of riding his tongue protrudes between his strong, widely spaced teeth. Neither he nor his son say a word. Our eyes cannot see to the end of the avenue stretching away straight as an arrow. It is early morning. It would be our horses' morning exercise. Aside from the high, indescribable pleasure, we would also have the satisfaction of performing a piece of work, of doing something useful, which was also appropriate to our name and our birth. Is there a more modest wish? Can anyone accept the "gift of life" with deeper gratitude? Does anyone see the necessities and superfluities of social being more soberly, if as greatest desire he longs for a simple hour's riding with his father, the impoverished prince without a position, in the avenue of a public park? But the prodigious value of being together with my father exists only for me. What I hope for from this hour with him (in vain, let me say immediately, it is past), it is nothing more than what all other sons always possess and never value. I was an orphan, when my father was still alive.

The most blissful condition is that of the beast, assuming that the stones and breezes are not even more enviable. Yet even the beast, in whose soul one can, even if with difficulty, place oneself, knows nothing of D. before it dies. I love horses, I love animals above everything, but something of this love is envy. The closeness of an animal, especially a beautiful, big, strong one, does me good, I bask in its presence. When my glances meet the eyes of the animal, I would like to become the little reflection in the horse's angular pupils, which look as if they are surrounded by crumpled brown vellum, or even live as a tiny Orlamünde in the satin-lustre eyeball of a cat, stretching and contracting in the light, as if it were a breast, that breathes in light and breathes out light.

So deeply would I wish to sink into the existence of an animal and dissolve there, where there is no more D.

For an animal, life is something prodigious. It does not comprehend D. at all, in that it remains for ever child, even the most doleful, the most tormented. Even the weariest cab-horse, which has become so weighed down on its bent knees, that no one who had known him in his youth, as a foal, would recognise him again, even he consists only of life without shadow of death.

In nature, life is hard for every animal, it struggles to find sustenance, but it has its whole strength for that. It behaves as if there were never a time to come, in which it no longer needed to search out its sustenance, because it itself would have become the sustenance of beasts of prey or worms. It seeks out its sexual partners for the first time as if it could anticipate them another thousand times, and so on until the last time with an equal pleasure, with the same deadly will. So an animal is more faithful and stronger than the most faithful and strongest man and more courageous.

When it enjoys, it enjoys gloriously all the delights of existence. So a cat sleeps on a wheat field which has been harvested, but on which the sun is still shining brightly, after it has filled its stomach with field mice or even with grasshoppers and has drunk the evening dew from a few cupped leaves. The cat lies there, its front paws folded under the calmly breathing breast, as if it were praying to itself. It has curled its tail around itself, as if for warmth. It has closed its eyes, indeed, it cannot get enough darkness and it tucks its rounded head deeper into the folds of skin of the neck. It rests. It is immortal. Is it not more enviable than any man? What is D. to it, what is life, what are father and mother? To me it is enviable, to me, who could never envy any man, even Napoleon. Yes, in its innocence before D. an animal goes still further, even if rarely.

I knew a magnificent tom cat which had the singular habit of going into fire. It was rust red in colour, had luxuriant hair, fluffy around the throat, matted on the belly, a very long neck and extremely strong, arched buttocks, which were, however, almost hidden by the huge brush, thick as a child's arm, which flicked back and forward like a tiger's tail. When I saw the animal for the first time, I noticed bald patches. They were round holes almost eaten or stamped out on neck and back, under which the clean, much licked skin shone through bright and pink. We took this to be mange, and did not touch the animal with bare hands, did not, however, stop it from rubbing and purring against the bottom of our trouser legs with its otherwise long-haired, finely rounded back. The tom cat only too gladly flattered my friend and me with its attentions, as if it felt that we, unlike most of the pupils at Onderkuhle, liked cats.

One evening in winter we were sitting in our room (actually it is mine only, but it does me good to share it with Titurel), in our dark, well heated room, my many desks gleamed, gently lit up from below. Light also came through the cracks in the door from the neighbouring dormitory, soft delicate lines which were only blocked out when one of our comrades walked across the room, without shoes, so that we could see rather than hear him.

Titurel and I, however, were alone, except that our cat had hidden itself away somewhere in the bottom drawers of a very old desk smelling mustily of classroom. We had made a bed for it there, from old exercise books, torn gloves and similar rubbish, which seemed to give it particular pleasure, even if it did not stay in it long. For there is something else that attracts it. We are talking about horses, examinations, teachers and pupils. Then we hear a strange chattering. The tom cat has come close to the iron fender, then it vigorously flicks its magnificent tail, whose erect hairs shine brightly in the glow of the fire, now the animal stands up on its hind legs. The sight of the strong rust red tom cat with the bare streaked patches on the supple arching back is terrifyingly beautiful, especially when the already blueish mass of light given out by the glowing coals falls on the long shimmering hair. Stretched out in this position the animal looks quite enormous. Titurel and I grasp each other's hands and squeeze tightly as a sign to be quiet and not to disturb the animal. At such moments it is hard for my friend to suppress a hoarse, sardonic laugh. But he understands my wish and forces himself to be silent.

Now that the draught has lessened, the flames have lost something of their brightness, have become blue-green, little clouds the colour of precious stones, more a deep haze than a burning mineral. We both feel its sultry, satiated breath as we kneel, open-mouthed, shoulder pressed against shoulder and neck against neck, in front of the fireplace. I look at my friend and see what, until now, he has always hidden from me, his carious teeth. For a moment he has forgotten them. Mouth gaping he wants to see how a beautiful animal struggles with D. But it affords me an indescribable feeling, a mixture of joy, shock, pity, affection, aversion and brotherliness, to see these yellowish teeth close to my snow white ones. Titurel's teeth have dark, chipped edges and small holes with gold fillings which catch the firelight and sparkle – I tremble when I look at this secret usually hidden from me, something in me grows strong and big, when he, Titurel, becomes small, earthly, mortal and fragile. I am only afraid that he notices and flees from me. For whom do I have here besides him? I have quite forgotten the cat and paid no attention to the harsh, throaty cry, to the reddish shining shadow of the animal as it leaps away – but all the more terribly does fear take me by surprise and cause me to call out loud, when I see my friend thrust his left arm, on which he has pushed the sleeve up to his shoulder, with the speed of lightning into the black mouth of the fireplace, its darkness still spitting sparks, biting back the pain, literally biting it back between his grating teeth. With all his strength he pulls the wretched animal out. In the fireplace it has puffed itself up enormously. It has tensed its muscles to the utmost. It struggles against its rescue, snarling and spitting, its jaw open, its nostrils drawn back and wrinkled. It has to be dragged out, its hind legs firmly held above the knees, and all the time it is crying with mouth wide open, as if it had been intoxicated by the flames as if by fresh meat, or become inflamed by a bloody carcass somewhere in the wood. It is indeed inflamed, for the stiff, curly, long, thick fur on its back is in several places glowing like paper which burns easily even though it is a little damp. Now it is silent, but is writhing frantically. Titurel wraps it inside his dressing gown, and in his impatience to stifle the flames and rescue the animal he also pulls out a corner of his white shirt, on which are printed plain aquamarine horseshoes together with crossed whips, and puts the strangely patterned piece of linen around the animal, quickly extinguishing the flames.

At my cry the comrades in the dormitory of the "Fifth" have become very quiet. We two, Titurel and I, are afraid that the horrible moaning of the burnt animal, which has to pay for its fire mania with fire wounds, will immediately resound in the silence. But not at all. Certainly the angry lascivious movements of the cat continue so violently underneath the protection of the shirt, that Titurel has to let the animal out. But it seems to triumph over D., over real death.

Who would not wish to change places with such a fearless being? The fire in the hearth flares up again, the voices in the next room grow louder. The cigarette smoke seeps in gently to us.

The tom cat opens its pink red mouth, shows its rough tongue, touched by a little milkiness, and yawns loudly. Purring, it rubs up against our feet, pushing hard against them with its high round forehead, and prevents us walking in a straight line to the window and letting out the air which smells sharply of singed fur.

6

The evening with the fire cat was the last that I spent with Titurel in my small narrow room that winter. Shortly afterwards he became ill, was given leave to go home to recover, and returned to us in late spring not quite healed. He has been brushed by D., one can see it on him.

Now it is perhaps time to say something else that also relates to D., but is quite opposite to it. I have already hinted at it, when I spoke of the fire cat. It made a deep impression on me. More than that: there was something about it, for which my soul had already long been prepared and which this courageous, painless, literally fiery animal, which defied suffering, confirmed for me. For there are times in my life when I am so filled with courage and vitality that, no less brave than the fire cat, I would like to throw myself into the flames. At such times I fear no danger, am without hesitation, I live with such fierce enjoyment, with such a complete satisfaction of all lust for life, that anyone who has known me only in the days of D., does not recognise me again. When in these days and nights of D., my wretched person has disappeared and has been nullified, so everything else alive and worth aspiring to in the whole world was also nullified with it. Since yesterday, however, since the little drive to the lake, everything in me has changed.

Now I am on my way to see my sick friend. I breathe so deeply that the silvered buttons of my uniform jacket are pushed out, I step firmly on the gravel path to the infirmary, so that it sounds like the clink of spurs (I never wear spurs, not even when working), I leap up the very bright, blueish whitewashed stairs to the hospital rooms, throw my pike grey cap on to the bed of the sick Titurel, placing the gloves inside it. I stand by the ivory coloured enamelled sick bed in a military posture, as if I really were the riding master for whom I am deputising. My hand touches Titurel's brow, which is traversed by vertical creases and on which ones sees, sharply marked, the cap rim as dividing line between the more and the less tanned part of his freckled face.

Despite the two open windows there is a strong sour smell in the room. But in me delight at life beats with a force I cannot describe and which I also cannot conceal from him. It is just this wild, almost painful surge of joy which makes me gentle towards him. What if this strong, sour smell comes from his mouth, nothing holds me back from bending over his drawn face and talking to him as if I were his elder brother. He does not reply. I thank him for the service with the gloves, but while I am speaking I cannot avoid turning my gaze towards his naked feet with their coarse-grained, horn-like toenails. Human feet have always caused me to laugh, they appear to me like caricatures of human hands. No matter how much I try to resist it, a smile, which he understands immediately, crosses my lips. For he turns pale with anger, doubles up his long torso, draws in his knees. He fixes me with his feverish, metallically glinting eyes and says in an impassive voice, without any trace of intimacy, "Quite superfluous. I am not responsible. The Master of

32

Ceremonies knows your circumstances." And as he presses his lips together, at the same time, with manly self-control, not returning his poor body to the comfortable position, he adds ironically, "You two . . ." but does not finish the sentence. He closes his eyes, pulls a handkerchief from under the pillow, folds it, places it on the night table beside the glass of water, in which the thermometer has been immersed. For him I am no longer there.

Yesterday he sat back to back with me on the gig. He saw the Master, as the latter bent down for my gloves. Today he, Titurel, would gladly have seen me bend down in front of him. Good. But in me there is such a joy in living, such a strong vibration to the ends of my hot and blissfully full veins, that I can feel nothing but joy, even now at the bedside of my only, sick friend. In his sense of injury I feel his love.

I stand up, fetch fresh water for him, put the thermometer back in its metal case, let down the blinds as quietly as possible, glance at the temperature curve carefully plotted by the college doctor (he is also our natural history teacher). I look at my Titurel. I take hold of his hands, which feel like a piece of warm meat. My only desire is to treat him like a child, a foolish, ignorant, unfinished, helpless, but greatly loved, being. Too gladly would I like to do something good to him, against which he cannot defend himself. He lies there silently, looks through me.

I am old beyond my years, I always felt it, now I know it. I am very alone here. I always knew it, now I understand it. No parents, no family lived with us in Onderkuhle. Whom should one love or hate? Can my friend Titurel take the place of a brother for me? Can the Master be a father to me?

Nowhere have I really put down roots. One only puts down roots if one starts out on a career, or earns one's bread by the labour of one's hands. Nobility isolates; who knows that better than I? Work binds.

Now, however, I live carefree in the college, I am not exactly a burden to this rich house.

I am not completely lonely, I am a piece of Onderkuhle. I too have a share in the school's blue flags, in the air, in the air of youth, the breath of boys all around our house, in the tall, beautiful forest stretching to the lake, which is no longer on our land, but already on the neighbouring domain of Squire P., a former pupil of Onderkuhle. These are the last days I am allowed to linger here.

Now as I step into the courtyard, paved with red, dry, clean stones, out into the bright sun, there is no trace any more of what I could have called the mark of D.

I feel so young, so strong, that for me at this moment there is no D., and neither for my friends, my loved ones, nor for my father, the old prince with the drooping lower lip, nor for my dear, gentle, shy, playful little mother, nor for my good friend Titurel, for my dear horses, for my teachers, for my fellow pupils, down to the very youngest, whom I hardly know. They have only just entered, they all huddle together, sullen and nervous like young goats, dispirited by homesickness and constantly fearful of nocturnal "tests". I resolve to touch them with especial tenderness, to treat them gently at fencing, at swimming and riding, when I deputise for the sick riding master.

My freshly washed gloves nestle softly in my hand, they lie warmed beside my cap, which despite the bright sunshine I do not put on. I am no longer ashamed of my unsightly hair, so much am I at home here.

Today the sun radiates something intoxicating, stupefying, it attracts me, it draws me upwards, to where among dark, violet clouds, it only shines down all the more brightly, prodigiously and at the same time more comfortingly on me and mine on this unforgettable June day.

7

In front of the infirmary I meet the Master. He, the most subtle eye, the active will in our house. One cannot even call it presumption, if he has taken over the actual management of all affairs, aside from teaching of course, for the Colonel (the Headmaster) quite gladly yielded it to him or even forced it on him. Now the Master stands in front of me. Does he take it as a sign of my inner superiority, when I first cover my head with my pike grey cap, in order then to raise it to him with a great sweep? So I, an Orlamünde, stand there bare-headed. He turns to me, bends down, although I am almost the same height as he. First of all he asks me, whether I can devote another year to Onderkuhle College. He takes my silence for assent, which it is. Then comes an important task, about which he begins to speak. Do I dare to take the horse Cyrus on the double lunge, since according to the groom he refuses to submit to any constraint and has already unseated one rider (the least skilful admittedly) with such force that the latter dislocated his shoulder.

At this question I am overcome, I begin to quiver, to tremble inwardly with bliss.

"I am grateful to you," I said, "I shall attempt it." The conversation is at an end, but the Master does not leave me.

He remains standing before me and stares at me; I remain standing before him and stare at the sun.

The sun is bursting out between clouds which have assumed the fatty blackness of negro bodies. But these clouds constantly and fearfully evade the ascending sun and form only a broad, monstrously sombre corona around the glittering star. The courtyard spreads out around me, as still as the grave. There is an extremely strong, but aromatic, smell of warm, heated stones, faded linden blossoms, of oats and refuse, it is as if the sun is enticing the smell out of everything in the strongest possible concentration. Never before in my life have I so hungered for dangers, into which I could throw myself, for pain, in order to withstand it by virtue of my irrepressible, furious vitality. Perhaps other people laugh when they feel something like it inside them, I control my face, I am silent and stop my mouth from moving. I merely stare at the sun, impudently, untiringly, unflinching. Up there the mass of light heaves in a flat, limitless bed. No boundary, no shore can be reached, it rises, it flows, a flood surges down from above the radiant brick-red roofs of the stables, in extravagant fullness it shoots down through the still, crowded, young linden twigs into my wide open eyes. Does one call it dazzlement, if today my eyes are able to catch the sun more clearly than ever before? My eye begins to spin. Wherever it turns, nowhere does it now find anything to fix on to, nowhere a sky any more, nowhere the black pile of clouds, nowhere now the low roof of the stables or the still steeper one of the school building, nor the branches of the trees of the avenue which leads to the lake.

I have quite forgotten what has so often dismayed me, the vast distance, the millions of miles of the avenue stretching from our poor earth to the sun's oceans of light which no human foot walks on. The "insane" temperature of 23,000 degrees which is supposed to reign up there, appears quite insignificant and petty to me now. It reigns over us in the most literal sense, we who hardly dare to raise the humblest glance to the unbearably powerful star. Who is an aristocrat compared to the sun? But now I dare to. No terror strikes me. No pain makes me flinch. No fear whispers to me, "Go and hide!" And yet once, at night, even the mere thought of this vast star was enough to make me, a child then, feel all the terrors of death and extinction. It was a bright night, snow had fallen. In the semi-darkened room at home I was given up, helpless and defenceless, to the idea of infinity. In vain did my unfinished, long, pale hands clench tightly between the dark *portières* of cheap, prickly velvet. I wanted to get a purchase on something in the bottomless depth of these millions of miles, which open up beneath all of us as an unsuspected abyss. For now, at this night hour, the sun is beneath us. All the endlessness of the universe is ready to swallow us up. Indeed, it has already swallowed us up, the emptiness has no end, only our life one day. In vain do I press my feet flat against the lower end of the bed, the coldness is only all the more awful and makes the sleepless, pathetically weak boy shudder.

It was the time when I was still sleeping in the same room as my dear parents, placed between the beds of my father and mother, for we have only one heated bedroom, the other rooms (nine!) are used for visitors. At home, if it is not very cold, a bed is made by our old Flemish servant David on a crescent shaped sofa in the dining room, but on such cold nights as this it is put up for me in the "tempered" bedroom. Excellent is the stove, homely, familiar, never over-heated, good to touch.

I, however, have abandoned it; overpowered by tiredness I am abandoned. My hands grasp hold of the fringes of the *portières*, which usually disguise a door, but the thought of D. bursts forth ever more terribly, it grows from inside and is not to be suffocated. What good is it if my parents rest beside me breathing evenly? They have reconciled themselves to everything, they have even accepted their "princely distress", suffer less than the servant David, who has served three generations of Orlamünde. Admittedly he is a Protestant, sectarian and cantankerous, my parents are sensitive, have "understood too well". So they may also long ago have accepted this dreadfulness of the universe as irrevocable. They have perhaps never been aware of it. Perhaps *I* am the only one who is crushed by this dreadfulness of sun, night, the numberless stars of the sky, like a linden leaf, which a falling rock of 23,000 tons in weight reduces to absolute nothing. But if this rock, this heavy, dead, immeasurable stone has tumbled down upon me, why does it not annihilate me completely with this one blow? Why for the whole of my life to come must I look D. and the absolute nullity of my existence in the eye and yet can never do so?

But today I can do so. Only today do I understand it, on the 19th of June 1913, at eleven a.m., now that I stand high above D., as I stare unprotected at the blazing sun with the greatest degree of optimism. Let it rage and storm, let it overflow, I say to myself, let it bubble over like a pot of milk on the hearth with its light and its heat, it may be larger than I, but not stronger, not today.

Beside the sun's immense body the Master has become a shadow, transparent. My wide open eyes no longer let out the sun, my head begins to sparkle, the reddish strands in my hair are about to burn and the yellowish ones to curl up – or will they turn white at this hour which will never return? I control myself. All mastery begins with self-control. I do not move. May I be burnt up completely in these flames of the sun. So shall the inevitable consume me in the struggle of youth. Better so, than to timorously succumb to D., which with shadowy hands catches even him who tries to hide himself away. All better, than to timorously submit to spiteful death. If one must be the rider and one the horse, then *I* shall ride and not spare the spurs.

8

The Master has disappeared long ago, to give the stable-boy the order to double lunge the horse Cyrus and take me to the "green" riding school.

I am still standing there in the quiet infirmary yard, I breathe in the sun and am intoxicated by it, as I have never been intoxicated by wine. I feel it like a sweet heaviness in my knees.

The fire cat has now approached me, purring metallically. With its dull coat it has stretched out over both my shoes. Now the holes are completely filled out again, the hair, standing up stiffly in countless points, crackles in the glaring, palpably hot sun, the cat's strong body quivers, the purring gets louder, as if something were cooking inside the magnificent, fiery, young animal. The voices of the younger schoolboys reciting their exercises in the main building, now sound faintly across the deserted courtyard from the open classroom windows.

The school, which emerges beyond the lime trees as if above slowly ebbing waters, rises higher and higher in the intoxicating sun from its quite insignificant hill. The clouds form a black, heavy, gloomy ring around the house that is my home. They have now taken the sun right into their midst. One no longer suspects it there, it is as if earth has been shovelled over it. A cooler breeze is blowing from the rustling lime trees, from the beginning of the Italian avenue. A well starts to splash, fresh water is being pumped for the horses. Two turkeys fight one another on the farm next to the complex, squawk loudly, fall upon one another, as if each wanted to ride upon the other, they beat their wings, whirl up dust, and through the dust fly pointed and brightly coloured feathers.

The interior of the "green" riding school lies in deep shadow. It is called green to distinguish it from the other, which is called the Spanish riding school. Even the oldest pupils don't know the reason. It is forbidden to ask. The Master has forbidden all of us to address the teachers without permission, and this prohibition is the real reason why we pupils stick together so closely.

Inside, the two riding schools look almost identical. The walls are panelled to a height of six metres or more and in addition to that, covered with thick plaits of straw which has already turned dark yellow. The green *manège* is oval in shape, the Spanish one is rectangular. Now, in summer, the covered riding schools are little used, but in my case it cannot be avoided. The main door is locked, the Master has taken charge of the key. The stable-boy on duty leads the horse in for me through a side entrance under a raised *portière*. Even the rustling of the thick, heavy material makes the strong, tall horse restless. He is already making little nervous jumps on the tanning bark which covers the floor of the school. Naturally I know the horse, a beautiful, mouse-grey stallion, a little over seventeen hands, with a blaze, a white fist-shaped patch on his forehead and dappled front legs. He looks as if he had stepped in milk. He is well-bred, a cob, his powerful, rock hard masses of muscle are loosely covered by very delicate skin, which one could notch with a needle. Proudly he bears on his swan-like, erect, rather long neck a triangular skull tapering very sharply towards small, tender nostrils. His pointed, restless, wing-like little ears twitch at the least sound, even when his own hoof strikes a pebble or his tail swishes against the *portière*. Noticeable is the broad, projecting chest, with the forelegs set wide apart and, by contrast, as if beaten into place with a hammer, the compressed rump with the full, huge haunches.

Now the horse keeps his head still. He does not whinny, nor does he champ the bit. The eyes are almost fixed. The upper row of eyelashes is beautifully shaped, each lash lies next to the other soft as silk, each one slightly curled as with a beautiful young human. The lower row, however, has gaps, only a few stiff, bristle-like lashes are irregularly inserted in the black lower lid. The horse's gaze is directed at my hand. The stable-boy and I now make the double lunge ready for the horse.

Every rider knows that the simple lunge consists of straps which are lightly, but firmly, attached to the chest of the lunged horse, in order to make the horse go round in circles as if it were on a lead. This is how it becomes accustomed to a regular, firm pace and to a particular bearing, the limbs being "gathered" under the horse's body. From then on the "paces" should shoot out with precision, covering ground with stride lengthened to the utmost; the right hindquarters in particular, which by nature step outwards a little, must be brought in and controlled, so that the mount can carry the weight of the rider at every speed and pace without any stiffness of the neck, back and hindquarters. Given the limits of the aptitudes of the animal and also of the teacher, this can usually be achieved without difficulty in the course of a regular breaking in.

The double lunge is different. Here a trammel is placed on both sides of the animal. It is of necessity connected to the bit, therefore to the head and to the spinal column, and indeed part of the harness goes from the right hand side of the mouth to chest height, goes from here to my hand and then back to the hindquarters of the beast. The other part of the double lunge is attached on the left hand side in just the same way. It is limp and ineffective as long as the horse obeys. If he withholds obedience, however, then this part comes into action and exerts control over the horse thanks to a tremendous leverage. From the point of view of the rider, the horse has duties just like a man and the animal also understands and learns this just as we learn our exercises and duties in Onderkuhle. Sometimes force is necessary with a horse as with a man. Who knows that better than I? For a long time one tries kindness, for the horse is, in himself, no wild animal, against which one must fight. At the beginning the horse does not know what a whip is, and so does not flinch from it. So no whip at the beginning! In his youth every horse is frightened by the unfamiliar pressure of the bit and with a terrified expression on his face tries to turn back, as it's called. So first of all one always tries to do it gently. One knows that a young animal's mouth is soft, its character inexperienced, childishly naive. One first applies a "soft, coaxing hand" – in vain with Cyrus. The riding master has pulled up whole beds of carrots and often filled his pockets with sugar. It was no use. He talked to the animal. The animal did not submit. Does he not want to? Is he unable to? What remains now apart from force? But if one uses it, and where it is absolutely appropriate, there one cannot shrink back from any means. For me personally reservations against the "torment" of subjugation could nevertheless perhaps arise in times of D., also I have never found such violent means necessary before.

Here, however, indulgence is no help at all. Now at the moment when life is at its brightest I shall achieve what I want. I control myself, therefore also others. If ever, then I know now, that there are forces which no living creatures can defy. If the horse suffers discomforts – one should not forget, I love horses with all my heart – and yet: if the horse suffers discomforts, constraint and pain, then in this case it has inflicted them on itself.

At last the harnessing, which is made more difficult by the restlessness of the horse and must be carried out with double the usual gentleness and care, is completed. I can let out the stable boy. I do not like witnesses. I must know that I am alone with the horse. So I remain alone with Cyrus, for that is the beast's name – have I mentioned it already?

It is fairly dark in the hall. Only from the ceiling, as through a church window, does a ray of light break through a ventilation flap. The sun has abandoned the mass of black cloud again. I proceed to the middle of the riding school and urge Cyrus on, first by shaking the loosely held lunge reins, then with shouts, to which Cyrus responds only by pricking up his little ears, and finally by firmly stamping my heels, which is supposed to lay down the pace to the animal, to get a move on and begin with the work. The horse is not "reined in". Admittedly he gets going at a rapid, irregular, stumbling trot, but not round to the right as he should, but after a few proper steps along the wall, he turns around in a flash, as he wishes, and tries to break away in the opposite direction.

If we were now on the road, for example on the way to the lake, with fields on either side, where people, automobiles, grazing animals can appear unexpectedly, then I would have to give way and let Cyrus have his will. For he has a will. He looks at me boldly, turns his milky forehead to me, blinks with his big stone grey eyes, which look as if they have been polished, and raises his white dappled legs even higher. They shoot out in magnificent motion beneath the supple body, which contracts rhythmically from left to right as he steadily continues in the wrong direction, stamping lightly on the bark, bearing his bushy tail raised high behind him like a grey flag.

Why not let him be? Is it worth breaking the will of such a beautiful, proud animal? That is the question of every education, including mine. Why not accept the false progress of D., which after all only appears false to us, the victims, and leave it at that? But is the recalcitrant man or animal then at least left in peace? Not Cyrus. The following course of action will and must be taken with him. If I have to give way now, the animal will never learn. He is useless both as a work horse and under the saddle and in our commercial age even the most beautiful animal is not maintained with such a great investment of effort and money, only for the sake of its beauty. On the contrary it is the case that the horse will be shot by the economically calculating Master, if he will not submit, and if my attempt fails.

The Master will then have the superb horse led to a grass-covered little slope, will draw a handy, hardly more than thumb-sized revolver out of the holster, which the proud grey beast sniffs with curiosity. The stable-boy, trembling with fear and dripping sweat with excitement, will hold a last carrot at the animal's teeth, in order to distract its attention. Meanwhile, the Master, careful not to touch the hairs of the ear and make Cyrus restless, has brought the weapon to the pricked wing-like gateway to the body – and as the horse snaps at the carrot, the weapon goes off in its ear with a soft, dry bang. The animal looks round in surprise at the sound. The boy believes the weapon has failed. He grips the reins again. (For the sake of economy merely a wretched, worn, death harness has been put on the horse.) But the Master pushes him violently away, for already the beast is going down on all fours, slides down the grass slope, like a piece of butter on a warm knife, and remains lying at the bottom so that the beautiful, triangular head with the white patch is lying on the slim, banded front hooves, like a dead grasshopper, his legs still sticking up, even though bent. The animal ends in this unnatural, graceless position. A neighbouring estate has a bone meal factory. Everything has already been agreed. The price for the bones will make good the fodder costs. A long, two wheeled open cart arrives from the estate. The animal dies, the Master calculates.

This end is hard for an animal lover's heart to bear. Should I not prefer a thousand times over to use my love of life for just a moment and win control over the animal, so that it may stay alive?

9

My first task is to remain standing motionless, unflinching and above all impassive in the middle of the room. The horse twists wildly. Without my intending it he has got messily tangled up in the reins as if in tethering ropes. The fine skin bulges out in swellings, whose edges, under the surface, immediately fill with pulsing blood, weals which will still be visible after months. Unavoidable. The horse cannot hold himself, he staggers, falls, he opens his mouth in astonishment. He does not whinny, however, he quickly wants to struggle up again. The floor of the high, oval space is shaken by the dull impact of the falling horse. The white patches on the forehead gleam with the violent movement. The horse begins to roll from side to side, to hide his head in the bark, but there is too little of it, again and again the horse's eyes become visible, and the eyelashes, already sprinkled with dirt, have lost their beautiful unbroken order. Lying there on his side, he whinnies and groans. But then he explodes, he shoots up from the floor, shaking up a cloud of brown dust, violently jerking his head, mechanically, angrily, unthinkingly. But he does not free himself. The steely rings of the well arranged and cleverly conceived bonds tighten once again, and it is as if nothing had happened.

At this moment it looks as if Cyrus would submit and now wanted to obey by trotting evenly in a rightwards direction. When he looks at me from the side, it is only to read my will in my eyes. Or am I deceived? Is it only guile? Malevolence? At every tenth step Cyrus rises up on his long hindlegs and comes closer to me, forces me towards the cavity of the oval wall, in order to strike down on me there. Is it too late, have I already allowed myself to be tricked by the malicious spirit? Did I, for the duration of a dearly bought moment believe that I stood, radiant in my high spirits, at the centre of the world, prevailing, because my horse has made a couple of regular turns around me.

Now that's finished with. Pushing himself up on all four legs from the bubbling, brown, steaming floor, he jumps to the left in skewed sideways leaps, at the same time throwing his head back with such an animal rage, that the bar which he has in his mouth strikes his teeth with a metallic noise. Suddenly, low, his limbs bent close to the ground, he moves through the *manège* with abrupt, lightning fast jumps. He plays with the double lunge, which has apparently lost all strength, like a child with a ribbon on its shirt.

Light penetrates the glazed opening in the roof, a strong silvery, gleaming beam as thick as a man. For the playing, raging animal I am no longer there. As little as for my only friend an hour ago. He plays with the ray of light, sniffs at it, dips his sweat-soaked, fluttering mane in the cone of light. The silvery hair of the mane sparkles close by the narrow white front bands, so oddly has the horse twisted round. He frees himself from this crooked position, making loud fa..s, draws his limbs together, jumps up, rises with all his strength and then lets his silky, shining, strong smelling, sweat covered body fall into the bark with a thump, as if he were playing with himself as with a ball. I stand there completely still, neither come closer to the horse, nor move further away from him. Despite the deafening noise, which the constantly whinnying and stamping stallion produces, I am as quiet as an hour before at the bed of my sick friend Titurel. The horse has now resolved on an impeded canter. At the same time it kicks out at the wooden wall with its hindquarters, that is, with both hind legs at once, having lowered its head right down between the braced front legs, and at each attack tears off some of the decrepit dark yellow straw wreaths. I hold the reins loosely. The high room echoes to the thundering noise.

I become all the quieter. I position myself firmly at an even more favourable spot, more towards the narrow side. I press my legs hard against one another, in order to gain as much support as possible. The horse watches me, imitates me and now stands still, drawing breath. That is dangerous. If the horse stands still, I have to move closer to it. If it is as clever as it appears to be, it can then smash my skull with one blow. Or it can throw its whole heavy body, dripping with sweat, filled with inner rage and tremendous violence, upon me and crush me. I once dreamed of such a death.

Whoever moves first is lost. I shall not be the one. We remain motionless for a quarter of an hour. The horse only quietly paws the ground, as if he wants to dig something up. The beautiful eyelashes of the upper lid shine bright as silk threads in the sun, like the ones my mother often lost out of her sewing casket. The horse breathes fast and loud through glittering, vibrating nostrils. The wet body dries quickly.

Then suddenly I throw the whip over Cyrus's back. I do not work with the whip. Rather with surprise. In its fright the horse has been forced to make a movement. It has lost its composure. And as, with elation, I hear the sound of trotting, I shorten the rein, at which the straps cut the inside of my hands despite the good strong gloves. The horse's trotting has now changed back to the familiar low canter again, round to the left; but what good does it do? Meanwhile I have properly arranged all four reins which lead from my hands. I feel the animal's every movement. I know now that the horse is firmly held by the double lunge. Now I raise both hands to head height and even higher, as far as I possibly can. I throw my body backwards. All the force of the animal's rhythm runs through me. In this way I have formed a lever. I have shortened the reins even further. So should my last and most important attempt fail, I have at least avoided the danger of being tangled up in the reins as in snares I have myself laid. The animal has felt my manoeuvres exactly. He still races on, circling the room with rhythmic whinnying and a stamping gallop. He continues to follow the forbidden direction to the left. He is experiencing the greatest excitement. The eyes shine brightly, almost like a cloudless moon. White foam drips between his teeth, flashing brilliantly in the sunbeam. Cyrus stretches his neck and half in anger, half in pleasure, throws his head from side to side as if it was hanging by a thread. Now I make a ninety degree turn. I have lowered the harness and wrapped it around my waist. The reins have been shortened by a half. This is the final struggle.

But I control the struggle. I control the horse. The inner rein is loose, although we have come very much closer. It is ineffective and cannot be effective, since the horse is being disobedient. But instead the outer one is taking effect all the more strongly and irresistibly with every step the horse takes. Already he is cantering more slowly, putting down smaller strides.

The struggling animal raises himself in his bonds of leather straps. His struggles make him defenceless.

Can that be? Yet it is so.

10

Cyrus feels the great strength in me. He has fallen silent. His hoofbeat sounds dully on the floor of the green riding school, broad swathes of which have been churned up. With bright eyes he looks at the inner rein, which hangs down loose beside the dripping mouth. He shakes it as if in play, as if he has nothing to fear from it.

But he is gradually being drawn in from the other side, from the "control" side. A tremendous leverage grows more powerful with every second. I am holding iron chains in my hands, but even more the animal is subduing himself. That is it. For through the methodical linkage of the reins the horse has pulled his nostrils back as if with a steel spring. A horse's nostrils, however, covered with the softest skin, are sensitive to the highest degree. Now, through his own unwilling strength, through his wanting to resist, he has tormented his most tender, most vulnerable, spot past enduring. For the nostrils are now pulled backwards as far as the nose band. Is it possible to watch that without trembling? Driven on by himself, the poor animal has imposed the most terrible pain, the most fearful twisting of his neck on himself. He cannot escape any more, even if he wanted to stand still. Suffering pains which are impossible to imagine and to know, the supple, mouse-grey neck bends like a bow stretched to the limit. Now it and with it the whole animal is like a twitching ice-grey pike, which leaps and arches up in the net and lacking water, defends itself desperately. But this is only the outward appearance. One sees only the surface. One cannot see inside Cyrus. But one can hear him. One can hear him, as he sighs. Wretched, piteous.

With the sound of the sigh, which is like the sound of a saw passing through fresh wood and which bears no similarity to the often inconsequential sighing of human beings, with this indescribable, unforgettable sigh, Cyrus's head turns in the required direction. Shyly and yet still full of strength, the body turns, the legs stretch and bend at a moderately fast trot round to the right, and with that the force relaxes. The most terrible pain must disappear. The animal obeys. He is so completely in my power, that I am ashamed of the fight. I am not yet completely free, but with a left turn of my body, can return to my earlier position, I can even move easily in a small circle. Now the "ordinary", the civil rein, I should like to say, that is the inner one, begins to take effect again. Now I relax the pressure of my hands entirely. I take a deep breath, I do not, however, look at Cyrus and know that he is not looking at me. The stable-boy has slipped in under the heavy *portière*. He now takes the horse out of my hands. Now he is obedient for ever. Only to one other sovereign will he have to submit after my sovereignty – to D.

Have I passed the test? Was it a test to the death? Have I passed it? Is it over?

Still in the cool twilight of the riding school the stable-boy rubs the horse dry with a towelling blanket. While the boy is busy at the chest, the horse sticks out his salmon coloured tongue, its tip still covered in white foam and licks the lad's hand.

I have just picked up the riding whip and wiped off the dust. I flick it at the pair of them and strike the tip of the horse's quickly recoiling tongue and the shoulder of the boy who flinches in fright. The light blow is hardly audible, and no sooner has it fallen, than I already feel deeply ashamed. A quiet round of applause, which is like a very belated echo of my blow, comes from the top lodge at the head of the riding school, where on festive occasions, equestrian tournaments and so on, the Headmaster, at the forefront of the teaching body, watches our efforts. Has the school not then been empty? Were there witnesses in the lodge? But one thing followed another so quickly, that I do not know whether the applause is for breaking in Cyrus, over which I would now most of all like to weep, or for the most thoughtless blow which an eighteen-year-old pupil and substitute riding master, intoxicated with optimism, ever dealt an innocent animal, only vanquished by mechanical means and barbarically crude pressures, and an able and willing, even if clumsy, boy. I do not turn round to the Master. He applauded. Nothing that is unjust can happen here in the house and outside on the farm, without him standing by approvingly and lending a hand for all his worth. He seems to countenance many of the pupils' dissolute habits, he encourages various of the Bookkeeper's rather opaque dealings. I am ashamed of his praise, I hate his unwanted, repulsive affection for me, although I owe my cost-free stay here to it – I and my poor parents with me ought to thank him on our knees.

Impossible. I bend down and brush the dust and scraps of bark from my knees with the back of my gloves. I was ashamed to say that earlier, during our unequal struggle, Cyrus threw me to the ground. With the reins around my body, sliding on my knees as if on sledge runners, he forced me to join in some part of his lightning fast criss-cross traversals of the riding school. At last the steps of the tired horse and of the stable-boy, stamping along like a peasant in his nailed shoes, fade away. Now the oval riding ground, every inch of which has been churned up, is empty. The sun breaks in from above with undiminished brightness, indeed at this moment, as I step out of the green riding school, raising my shoulders, it seems even to have gained in brightness and fire, size and brilliance.

I still have vitality in me, although I feel that I have not stood this test. I am now resolved never again to break horses in such a way. I never want to be a jockey, not a steeplechase rider or trainer, rather, if it must be, a lad in a stable, where the aristocratic animals, whose nobility is far superior to human beings, are cared for. If I must withstand tests in the struggle with D., let them be different ones.

Since it is midday by now, my comrades have repaired to the large courtyard for their break. They stand around in small groups. From a distance, in their loose, dust coloured, summer uniforms, they all look as alike as brothers from one house or sheep from one fold. They recognise me from a distance, call out pleasantries, not always of the most proper kind. A small boy asks me for help (but it is irony more than anything), as he is engaged in a fight with fat Prince X., whom we call Piggy. But there is no question of that. I hate Piggy, it is true, for in the "princes'" dormitory he told the low story which robbed me of my innocence with regard to D. But it would not be right to take sides in a fight between these boys. I pass them with a silent, tight-lipped smile and make for my room, to wash myself and to change my uniform, which has become soiled by dust and sweat.

11

Since the heat has become almost unbearable, the teachers have decided to cancel teaching in the afternoon periods. Its place is to be taken by physical exercises. And so one group, which includes the youngest pupils, is to play a kind of handball, a second group is to play tennis (both very foolish because of the unshaded courts), the third group, beginning with the "Fifth", that is, the oldest pupils, is being allowed to ride into the horse-pond with some horses.

The horses will be led out at four o'clock, without saddle and stirrups, bridled only with reins. We have to put on our bathing costumes, and over them, for as long as we are in the area of the farms, our grey gym clothes.

To ride on unsaddled horses is not always a pleasure, even for an enthusiastic horseman, and on leaving the water the horse must be ridden dry. That is hard work, for the horses are equally sensitive to both cold and damp, and given the prevailing humidity, this presents no easy task. Yet the satisfaction of a swim in the lake is attractive, as is the pleasure of spending a few hours without supervision by the teachers. For I have been chosen to be leader of the party instead of the riding master, and the pupils may safely regard me as their equal.

So the ever darker, gathering clouds, the low, threatening storm cannot frighten us, we may ride out even in the heaviest rain and remain outdoors. Admittedly not everyone is as delighted as I am by this plan. Young Prince Piggy, a small, fat, young gentleman with a creamy brown face (he was born in the tropics), with black eyes sparkling like cherry jam and a very pale, broad, even if extremely firm mouth, has not quite got his mind on the business at hand. Usually he likes to shout or let out his barking laugh at the most foolish excuse, now he's murmuring and whispering and seems to want to convince his comrades of something, which they, however, do not take seriously, for they pay no attention to his muttering. I cannot believe that it is lack of courage on his part, since neither in myself nor in others could I ever imagine cowardice in the face of everyday things (and those are, after all, water, storm, horse, thunder and lightning).

Now we all stand in front of the stable door with our loose unpressed gym clothes flapping around our ankles, to await the horses who are already stamping and pawing inside, tugging at the jingling spring-hooks and chains and whinnying softly. Their tails can be heard striking against the fodder racks, making a curious hissing noise, as well as the sound of their noses "rubbing out" the saliferous walls.

Suddenly, to everyone's astonishment, my friend Titurel crosses the now shadowy courtyard from the infirmary. He is still somewhat pale; but if one did not know, one could not tell the fever and sickness by the look of him. He joins the others, is dressed just as we are in grey-white gym clothes and has folded the towel, which is taken when we go swimming, over his belt. Since the number of horses is limited, one of the other pupils must forego the excursion if Titurel is to come. The school clock is just striking four. The animals are already crowding out side by side through the wide open door. Now the unsaddled horses, their soft bodies squeezing against one another, appear naked, lean and not so well-proportioned as is otherwise the case under the narrow, well-fitting pigskin English saddles and the broad, gently encircling girths. Who shall remain behind? Is Piggy really thinking of himself? He looks at me, whose decision it is. He tries to catch my glance. It is not clear to me how he does it, because he does not really fix me with his eyes, he maintains the proper comradely bearing, neither excessively self-confident, nor emphatically familiar. He has already taken his horse and is stroking the narrow rein with his strikingly feminine thumb. I already have his name on the tip of my tongue and want to ask him to stay behind, when I notice that he has sensed this, and that his fingers are about to let go of the rein again. So he really is a coward, he is afraid of riding an unsaddled horse (yet there is no second, unbroken Cyrus among these animals), he does not want to go into the water sitting on an unsaddled horse and entrust himself to a swimming animal. Precisely because I recognise his cowardice, I do not yield to it and ask the youngest among us, an especially gifted boy, who has been admitted to the ranks of the much older pupils because of his advanced attainments, to stay behind and to join his peers at play. He is a delightful lad, modest, lively, with a round red and white face, as if formed out of porcelain. Among us he is called Assissus, after the famous saint; how he came by this name I do not know. He was given it in my absence at night in the dormitory after a very harsh "test" which he bore without batting an eyelid.

I delay no longer, take over my horse, a fairly tall, elderly, grey mare, from the stable boy, grasp the rein with my left hand, support myself with this hand on the rounded shoulder and, my right on the croup of the horse, which is soft yet unyielding under my grip and with a leap which looks effort-less but is always difficult, throw myself across the animal, which I have given no time at all to think. I sit on top, reins in my left hand, belt buckle in my right, my legs firmly clasping the mare's naked body, while the others are still struggling with the jostling and now fidgety horses.

It is quite dark under the lime trees of the avenue, for the sky has become even more overcast since morning. The heavy, almost tangible aroma of the softly rustling lime trees, covered in honey-coloured flowers, mingles with the vapour rising from the many horses. Flocks of sparrows sweep chirp-ing down from the trees to the horses' feet, for they expect something there. The birds are unusually agitated. Again and again dull brown, puffed-up little wings can be seen, they have opened their paler beaks wide, and so they raise little clouds of dust in the middle of the road, they bathe in the dust until they flutter up in front of the horses, shrieking with excitement and pleasure. The storm is in the air.

My friend Titurel is the first of the pupils to succeed in finding a firm seat. Once there he stays silent, sitting very upright. He has stretched out his freckled hands and his forearms, which are covered in blond down, in front of him. So he remains beside me and waits, until with loud laughter which only makes the horses even more restless, all the others have climbed up too. It takes a long time, for each boy tries to help the other, finally there is only a mass of impatient, sweating and urinating horses, of grey gym suits already darkened by sweat under the armpits, of boys' hands, at which the horses' mouths tug, and of boys' faces, which are bright red, partly from laughing, partly from the effort. Only one is pale, calm, stays aloof and smiles mockingly, even if almost imperceptibly with his thick lips and his handsome false cherry jam eyes: Piggy.

12

Now we begin to trot off at a very gentle pace. For it is not easy to keep oneself on top for any length of time, to maintain one's balance and to impose one's will on the animals without a saddle and especially without stirrups. Certainly one or two of the physically weaker boys would have been in difficulties, had not the horses, as truly social animals, followed one after the other, full of joy and pleasure, feelings which they demonstrate by constant whinnying, by raising their heads, pointing their ears and by a special dance-like, affected, unnatural gait. The warmth of the animal bodies passes on to us. Their soft, satin-like hairs rub against our twill suits. At each step our figures jerk up and down as if galvanised. So we come down the ever more strongly scented avenue of lime trees, almost completely dark under the storm clouds, past the school's playing fields, past the stables and farm buildings. Now we cross a little bridge which echoes dully under the many horses like the drum of a wild Congo tribe.

In the orchards all the blossom faded long ago. Now a strong, hot wind begins to spin and whirl the leaves round and lift them upwards. The foliage of the trees has taken on a bright green sheen. The trunks seem formed from a stick of tobacco, so dull and saturated are they in their blackness under the dark, blue-lined storm sky. I turn round to my companions, who cannot all follow me equally quickly. I catch sight of our school building, which seems to stand out all the taller and mightier against the sky, the further one draws away from it. Against the background of dark clouds, its usually raw red colour has been transformed into something more delicate, strawberry coloured, into something gay, despite the sombre atmosphere. I feel with a special happiness how beautiful our house is, how solidly built, founded to endure for ages. Shall I grow old in it, always live there?

The regular trotting of my grey mare is very pleasant. When a hoof strikes a stone, it goes right to my heart, I am so happy. If Titurel, his pointed elbows sticking out a little, comes close to me as we ride, it is as if he's stroking me; despite his still aloof, feverishly proud spirit, I feel his presence, his eternal being close by me. We shall grow old in our reticent friendship and quiet sympathy. Now, as the school lies behind us and we ride along beneath young beech trees, which only wave and whisper gently in the calm air, I feel myself as far removed from D. as never before.

Now comes the poplar avenue, which is called the Italian Avenue, beyond which on both sides there is a forest. It is still, even the gentle whispering has ceased, no bird call, only the regular trotting of our horses, who have found one and the same rhythm, the silvery jingling of the curb chains and the rustling of the pupils' clothes and the heavy breathing caused by the difficult manner of riding. No one is talking any more. At the start I heard laughter behind me; Prince Piggy's barking laughter, which was broken up by the gait of his jogging horse. Now, this too is at an end. The horses' pace is gentler, they step on the grass at the roadside, they also do not avoid the damp earth, and they thought-lessly crush under their hooves the tall docks which have shot up to giant size here. This is not without risk, however, since remnants of the prickly heads can accumulate in the bend of the joint behind the hooves and cause malanders, a bad foot infection. So I ride along the length of the column and give the younger riders support by bringing their horses, despite their reluctance, back to the roadway. The boys look at me, they smile, sweat drips from their happy, healthy faces, one or other of them trying to catch it with an upward curl of the lip. In vain do they try to soften the somewhat violent jolts, yes, they would not be disinclined rather to let the horses go into the dangerous burdocks if only it would mean less pain for them. But I am responsible for both, for the horses as for the boys, I am here among them in place of an officer, not quite as comrade.

Now the track is uphill, towards the small lake. Here there are beeches, oaks and amid the lighter, downy, milky foliage appears the serious, metallic green of the conifers, on whom, arranged like fruits, shine the pale green new shoots. A dark, almost black sky drives the crowns of the trees, trembling in the breeze, together. Then the track opens out, the outflow of the completely black lake rushes in muted drum beat over the weir, freshly constructed a year ago of white, planed tree trunks without bark, to which moss and algae have as yet only attached themselves in thin strips.

At this point we turn off the road and ride across a mown meadow, in the middle of which some tall haystacks are piled up. They exhale an almost stupefying vapour under the now completely overcast sky. Only brief fragments of bird-song can be heard. Further away in the distance a herd of cattle is grazing. Many animals lie as if struck down, only feebly moving their jaws and expanding their ribs as they breathe.

A few, black and white ones, move slowly and lower their heavy heads with the curling grey and black horns. It is very still.

Titurel's horse, a young black stallion, has become restless. Pestered by midges, he now begins to swing his strong tail and, when this does not help, to dance with his strong buttocks, glittering like a dung-beetle's back. Each one of these movements causes Titurel, who is visibly exhausted, pain. Without speaking, I place my hand on the horse's head collar. The horse is about to quieten down, when Titurel roughly jabs the animal's side. Breathing more wildly and irregularly again, it immediately kicks out with its hind-quarters. I do not, however, let this duel continue any longer, but calm the animal with a low whistle and at the same time place my left hand soothingly between Titurel's knee and his horse's flank. So everything becomes peaceful.

Meanwhile the other lads have quickly slid down from their horses, some so clumsily that they roll over the soft, grassy ground and let themselves be dragged around for another minute by the playfully whinnying horses, who are at the same time jumping up in the air on all four feet, a game which is without risk, because the boys can at any time let go of the reins by which they are attached. Most of them quickly undress, that is, they throw their gym shoes, twill jackets and trousers in a heap and now stand there in their green and white striped bathing costumes. They rub their hands in anticipation of the swim, while the horses, equally impatient, nuzzle the boys' naked shoulders with their nostrils, and at the same time paw the grassy soil with their hooves as if pleading. Other pupils have amused themselves by fastening the horses in threes to a single halter, so that they cannot get far. Instead the beasts indulge themselves at the tall haystacks, they pull out bunches of grey-green fragrant hay, which has, however, already turned somewhat dull, and, without being really hungry, grind it slowly between their teeth, then, playing and fighting with one another, they throw themselves against one of the easily upset hayricks till it collapses and buries the animals, their eyes wide with astonishment, under the hay flying in all directions. Meanwhile the sky has grown ever darker. The rain must be very near, fish frequently jump above the lead-coloured surface of the water, which only appears lighter close to the shore. The birds in the nearby forest have fallen completely silent. A cow begins to low. The midges sing out, but now they cannot be seen.

All the boys are now wearing only their bathing costumes. We separate the fastened horses, mount once again and keeping a tight rein, ride slowly into the shallow water by the shore. The coolness of the water is a blessing for the animals. They whinny happily, trumpet loudly, they drink greedily. Then they go carefully into the water, they lift their legs high like prim girls. Their chests expand and they swim, they whip the water with their mighty tails, which spread out like fans.

13

There is a wild tumult on the lake. The boys laugh, splash each other with water, at the same time sheltering their cropped heads – gleaming under the almost nocturnal sky – behind the horses' necks, while with their bodies bent forward they also hold on tight to the horses' necks. The spinules of the boys' backbones appear as thick strings of pearls under the cotton material which slowly absorbs the water. Occasionally, the pressure of the water lifts a boy from a smooth horse back, and only with an effort does he regain his seat, looks round, his mouth still full of water, laughing with embarrassment, and is soon out in front of the others. Titurel stays by me on his black stallion which now, so it seems, has quietened down, His colour is good, his gaze is calm and free. He is just as I have known him for all these years. Algae with drops of water have become caught in the horse's eyes, green and glittering between the very close, rod-like protruding lashes. The animal shakes his head. Absent-mindedly, without looking properly, Titurel wipes the green weeds from the black, glass-clear eyes of the horse.

At this moment the storm breaks with a brief, sharp clap. Lightning and thunder simultaneously. The centre of the storm is directly above us. A mass of yellow sparks out of the middle of a livid cloud, bellied out by the wind, but behind which even taller, blacker clouds loom up. In the distance the surface of the lake until now lead-coloured, ripples in the storm as if a pale grey net was being drawn at great speed through the water. At the same moment it has already turned cloudy right down to the depths. It hisses up and begins to rise in large rounded waves as if it was boiling. All at once the boys' shouting and laughter is cut short.

I cannot understand why a thunderstorm frightens them. I love thunderstorms above all else. But the others have fallen silent. With pale, shiny faces, their eyes sunk deep in their sockets, their hands with the twisted reins mostly clenched tight at the breast, legs pressed tight around the bodies of the horses, they are suspended above the tall, wet necks which look as if they have been cut from enamel. The animals, since they feel safe simply because of their large number, are fairly calm and that is good. Titurel, however, is frightened to death. His face has a greenish pallor, almost like the green stuff which he tried to wipe from the eyes of his black horse. But worst of all, I see how, without realising it, he digs his fingers into the right eye of the poor horse, which with a huge leap, immediately breaks away from the shallower water by the shore and now, half swimming, half leaping, whips up white foam around his limbs. He plunges towards the deeper part of the lake. Now he no longer has the bottom beneath his feet, he swims away, is in deeper water, holds his head at an angle to the water and the storm black lake breaks pale against the sharp triangle of his neck as against the keel of a moving ship. But he still feels the burden on his back, he shakes himself, kicks out wildly. His tail whips up foam. Whinnying loudly, he raises his buttocks, resisting the rider, who now hangs from the horse more like a lifeless bundle of clothes, instead of controlling the animal by his seat. I can only watch him from some distance, since under the circumstances my own horse can only with difficulty be made to obey. Titurel's eyes are completely closed, now, evidently in a state of almost complete unconsciousness, his long body slides backwards, his head falls to the side. He tries to open his mouth to cry out, but between the repeated claps of thunder all that can be heard from his direction is something thin, feeble. His ear shines level with the buttons which fasten his bathing costume at the left shoulder, it is as if he were eavesdropping on himself.

I still cannot take it all seriously. Nothing has happened after all, not a drop of water has fallen from the sky. But now Titurel opens his pale, bloodless mouth very wide, his bad teeth are visible, his smile is terrible, for a sick, small child in its feverish deathbed fantasies smiles just so. With that he has also finally lost his hold. I still see, as my mare makes for the shore with all her strength, like the other horses, I still see, how with his tanned boy's hand, which is usually so strong, he strokes the dripping forelock of his horse which is swimming towards us. It is as if he were combing the fringe out of a lady's face, it is not as if he wanted and had to hold on to the horse's mane, until I hurry to his aid.

The thunder now rolls with full force across the empty surface of the lake and the tall trees waving in the wind. The rain bursts down with a crackle, as if it were being fired from above. Where it strikes the water, there is a white splash. It falls in such quantity, that one feels as if under water. No air to breathe. One can see nothing, hear nothing apart from the roar. There is a smell of sulphur. The horses cry out more than they whinny. The confusion is indescribable. I hear the younger boys weeping amid the tumult of the elements. Prince Piggy calls loudly for help, but it is only mockery, for immediately afterwards his barking laughter sounds from the shore.

Relieved, I want to take a deep breath. Nothing of D. But my alarm is inexpressibly deep, when, at the same moment, the smooth, empty back of Titurel's stallion emerges beside me. No trace of the rider. Not a second is to be lost. I have no longer to think of myself, neither of life, nor of D., only of the boys, for whom I am responsible. Coolness, courage, resolve! I detach myself from my horse, which shoots away from under me like a white fish. The water is a foaming mass, broken by countless splashes, warm and violently driven into strong waves. Titurel is nowhere to be seen. Can he already have saved himself? Has he made it ashore, to the uproar behind me? Has the Prince received him with his barking laughter? *Must* he not have been saved? A man does not go under without a sound. In myself, life is now so much stronger than everything else, that despite all fears, despite all the lightning flashes ripping open the sky between the cloud layers, despite the violet storm clouds, I would most of all like to cry out with happiness, I would like to roll around on my back, let all the power of summer and the warmth of the rain gush down into my eyes, on to my breast.

But when for half a second I catch sight of Titurel's thrashing feet, with their so familiar dark yellow toe nails, everything in me goes numb; the paler objects further away must be his hands, striking the water but not pulling against it. Then, however, with a muffled gurgle everything sinks in front of my eyes.

With a single vigorous swimming stroke I am beside him. Luckily for both of us the horses have left the water, they have all swum back. The surface of the water spreads out empty before my eyes, still half blinded by the torrential rain. Now I only see a whitish-green bundle floating under the waves. From the front, with my right hand, I grasp Titurel around the neck which he cranes towards me. I recognise immediately, however, that I can no longer swim. So I have to release him again. The rule, and this has been drummed into us, is: hold the drowning person from behind. Expect a struggle in the water. He clings on to my upper arms. Like this we are both lost. I must deliberately hold his mouth and nose shut, press the chin against the upper jaw from below with the palm of my left hand, pinch his nose together with thumb and index finger. I must push his face away from me. It must be done. I must brace my knee against his body. Now at last he let's go. Thank goodness! Quite coldly and clearly remembering the Master's lessons, I push him under the water again. I get a proper hold of him. He is already unconscious. His big, long, pale body, around which the puffed up swimming costume billows loosely, is without independent movement. I take his weight. In order to swim more easily, I lower my head into the water. Now it is a matter of perhaps a hundred correct swimming strokes, given a careful estimation of my energy and of how long I can hold my breath.

I see the shore coming ever closer, even if the rain blinds and deceives. The burden becomes ever heavier; let it be heavy, I have strength enough in my hands, which are parting the water, pulling at the water properly and then turning. I soon have the bottom beneath my feet. The bottom virtually thrusts against my toes. Now I am still staggering, the warm, strange burden presses my neck down and for the first time today I have to swallow water which then shoots painfully out of my nose again. But now I stand upright, and as sharp pebbles cut the soles of my feet, carry the unconscious, not breathing Titurel through the pattering rain, right through the reeds by the shore which are almost as tall as a man.

Only a few of the horses and boys are there. We lay Titurel down on one of the haystacks destroyed by the horses, trying as far as possible to turn up the dry hay. We begin at once with artificial respiration, while rain pours on to the boy's face, into his open mouth. His lips are just as pallid as the rest of his face. It does not take long for the artificial respiration to be successful, breathing begins, becomes faster and louder and young Titurel pushes his head back deeper into the hay, as if he was lying at home in bed and only wanted to rest more comfortably. But we do not leave it at that, we slap him with the palms of our hands, but strongly enough, on the side, and Prince Piggy, who has helped with everything, strikes the cheeks with his clenched fist, till they redden nicely. Then I hear a sigh, which sounds very like the one which the horse Cyrus uttered this morning at the double lunge. But this sound, which is like a saw drawn through fresh wood, does not shame me. It does not make me proud. Only calm. So then the two of us, the Prince and I, take the boy in our arms and bring him to the end of the lake, where the Master is already coming towards us in his carriage. There Titurel is bedded down well.

At the Master's question, the Prince explains the incident in a few words; the Master does not reply, is silent at first and then informs us of a great inspection, which is expected. Whether it is a general or the Minister of Education or the bishop or simply the Chief Trustee of Onderkuhle College, is not revealed, and faithful to our old custom, we do not inquire further. The Master takes off his waterproof coat, which is flannel lined. He covers the helplessly smiling boy with the warm, dry, yellow and red check lining of this coat.

14

I have already related that I ducked my friend under the milky, clouded water, spurting up in the rain, so that he lost consciousness completely, making rescue possible. But now I myself lose consciousness. Something stirs irresistibly in the secret recesses of my life. I can do nothing, but let everything pour over me. With a heavy heart, drawing ever longer, warmer, sweeter breaths, I surrender to it. What can I call it? It is the first time and yet so familiar, I cannot describe it. One does not experience this moment twice. I know the road, which our carriage now takes, very well. I have often driven a gig here. Every tree is known to me. I recognise each one under the waterfall poured down by the cloudburst. I am aware of each bend in the road, yes, all too aware, despite being dazzled by the ever more tumultuous descending storm, whose lightning flashes have become fewer and a gentle blue, but also unbearably bright. At the same time as I draw out my new happiness with my breathing, I measure the distance to our old school house, rising high above the dripping Italian Avenue in its deep, dull red. I can see all this clearly; but what I cannot describe is the bliss surging through everything, and filling everything, even the deepest, most secret chamber of my heart. There are no words, today I can hardly recapture at all what I experienced then. There are not many such days. It was something that had never been granted me before.

Outwardly it is an odd sight, perhaps far from agreeable to a stranger. A thin, apparently boneless, youth in a green-white swimming costume, with very thick, strangely piebald hair, the bare skin of face and hands buttercream coloured and full of freckles, the long sinewy arms wound round his friend's neck; his hands feel the pulse beats there and count them, as if they were all the years I would still live to see. On this day I have withstood two tests to the D.

So perhaps I appear to a stranger, Prince Piggy for example, trembling with excitement, lips pressed tightly together. He has been forced on to the front seat of the carriage by Titurel and myself. He stares boldly at us both with his cherry jam coloured eyes. He is fully clothed apart from gym shoes and cap. The torrential rain, the hot, heavy thunderstorm wind, strike me from every side. But inside me something stupefying, something irretrievably over-whelming, is occurring. My indescribable feeling of happiness makes me silent, weighs heavily on me.

So we drive wordlessly on towards the poplars, which bend in the storm wind, along the familiar linden avenue, whose trees seem to have increased beyond counting. The rain which pours down into my mouth and on to my face from the honey coloured, faded branches, tastes of linden bloom scent, of cool, flowery essences.

My friend is wide awake and warm. He sits up, glances round and draws the Master's coat more tightly around him.

PART TWO

1

At this moment on the unforgettable June day, the 19th of June 1913, the high point of my all too strong vitality is passed, and there begins something that is natural and yet so heavy to bear, the transition into times of D. I resist it. I struggle. But did I not already say at the breaking in of Cyrus, that his very struggle makes him defenceless? Can that be? Yet it is so.

Now I have returned to Onderkuhle with my friend Titurel. No one thanks me for having saved him. Yet the evident injustice makes me brave. I am only defenceless against kindness, gentleness and weakness. But neither the Abbé nor the Headmaster have seen anything but negligence in the whole affair. It does not surprise me that Prince Piggy is pleased at the cool reception. There is only one who stands by me, the Master, who signals to me with his hand, which is adorned with a precious green ring.

But what are they all to me, the Abbé and Piggy, the Rector and the Master? I shall disregard them and turn away from them, smiling silently. But something else strikes me grievously. I cannot disregard it, I cannot turn away smiling silently, if Titurel displays a hardly concealed aversion to me. He will say nothing unseemly, thanks to his education he possesses too much self-control for that. But yet he does not possess sufficient self-control to grant me justice. But then is it justice that I long for? One does not demand true affection nor give it either in return for payment and good reasons. Loving and being loved are either self-evident or impossible. What good are words? He does not tell me the reason, I do not ask him. I feel now, that if one has lived year after year, with a human being, an only friend, one who is irreplaceable, then understanding needs no words, or despite all explanation there is no understanding at all.

What remains for me? My future? New questions, insoluble ones. My parents, my father, my mother? I want to speak with them, to greet them, to know them close to me, to write to them, but I do not succeed in doing so. I write salutation after salutation, each one more affectionate than the other, but I do not feel any of them. Even the simple, unadorned "beloved parents" seems untrue to me. When I look up from my letter, I see Titurel and am happy, *that he is alive*. Titurel feels it and no longer allows me even this moment. He turns away, but looks malevolently up at me from the side and whispers, "Take care, if you ever lay hold of me again!" "I lay hold of you?" I ask. "Who allowed you to push me under the water? You want to show yourself off. Am I a stupid horse, on whom you can practise your skills?" I follow him, take him in my arms, draw him by the shoulders over the threshold once again and look at him. Never had I thought to humiliate him. To command others meant nothing to me. My only wish was to conquer the eternal feeling of D. and by withstanding tests to make myself free of the fear of D. I have loved this young man, not as one loves a woman, not as one loves one's parents, but as one loves oneself and one's own youth. I would gladly have lived close to him, known him by me. Now we shall no longer know each other. If he now leaves the room with drooping shoulders, with chin held high in rejection, he no longer reminds me of the only friend of my youth, he is my fellow pupil in the aristocratic school, not closer, not more a stranger than others.

Although I realise, before I fall asleep, that this is a final farewell, I am awakened less than an hour later by a quiet noise at the door and I persuade myself that only Titurel could announce himself to me in this way, that only *he* could return to me so swiftly. Yet I know that his way of knocking is different, two short, sharp blows. I should also have to tell myself that he, my erstwhile friend, would also step without knocking through the small connecting door, which leads from the dormitory of the "Fifth" to my room and not from the corridor, where at this time an orderly is always sleeping. Fortunately I control myself sufficiently, so that in the illusory joy of anticipation I do not address the figure coming closer to me in the darkness of the room as Titurel. It is not Titurel and never will be. I am silent. The Master too is silent. Then he sits down on the edge of the bed and begins to speak. I learn now who is awaited, the Duke of Ondermark, a famous explorer and former pupil of our institution. "And where will you go?" he asks abruptly. I am silent. "When I came here, my dear Lord Orlamünde, I thought it would only be one year. Do not ask me how many years it has become. I thought of making a small fortune, no matter how. Of founding a household, no matter where. None of that was achieved in time. I have become acquainted with many people here in the course of the years. Every six years everything is renewed. New faces, new voices, old names. Nothing is mine. I have grown grey." Since I am silent, he goes to the window. Outside the rain is falling with undiminished force. The water runs down, as if in thick columns, which hardly break up into drops at all, from a low sky, which strangely, is paler in colour. He repeats again from the window, "Where will you go?" "Where else should I go?" I say. "Here I feel happy." "Happy?" he says. "Does an Orlamünde live for his own sake? You shall know many here and have no friends, you shall give orders here and yet not command, you shall . . ." Suddenly he says in a changed voice, "You, an Orlamünde, surely do not wish to become such as I?" Outside the sky has grown much brighter, and I can see his sharp, wide-set, slate grey eyes in which an expression of self-annihilation is stronger than his love for me. He, otherwise always sovereign, has bowed down low. Now he pushes his hair very flat against the curved temples, so that in the dull light it shines in a mixture of grey and black next to his beautiful gems. He shakes his head slowly once again, as if to say: "Become a no one such as I . . ." Then he opens his mouth, displays his narrow white teeth, which have been preserved in the old mouth. He acts as if he quickly wanted to interrupt, were I to begin to speak.

I too could speak. There is much that I have told no one and which one can only tell a father. A father who is one's own flesh and blood or an adopted one. But I cannot do it.

I prayed with the others in the school chapel next morning. My place is no longer among the pupils, neither may I count myself among the teachers, so I force myself between both groups. The domestics, the teachers, the Bookkeeper, the doctor, the tutors and also the estate officials, whom we usually rarely see, are all gathered in the much too small chapel. Only one is missing, who otherwise had his eyes everywhere, the Master, who does not belong to our faith. During the sermon the Abbé repeats the names Father and Son again and again. The word father strikes me, as a blow from a hoof strikes one who is lying on the ground.

Expected, inevitable, dull and blind. He, the refined, but in his way cold and obstinate, priest, wrapped in his silk vestments, which even cover his hands, who utters these words up in his pulpit, does not know who is lying at his feet. It is not the letter from my father, awaited in vain for weeks, which could force tears from me, were it not that tears are unknown to me. For as long as I can remember, I have never wept. It is not the feeling of loneliness. It is something which one cannot properly think through to the end, still less express, one cannot concentrate, reflect on oneself. One may tell oneself to use the brief moment in which the slate grey eyes of the Master are elsewhere, to find comfort in this rare hour, to inwardly recover oneself and at last to come to a decision. Is there no weapon that could end the struggle between life and D. in me? Is there nowhere I can turn for advice? If my flesh and blood father is far away and remains silent, if my adopted father thinks only of success and action, endeavour and ambition – is there no one in whom I could confide? My heavenly Father? But what do the words "heavenly Father" mean to me? "Father" everything – "heavenly" nothing. Is what oppresses me so rare? Has it not befallen anyone else? It is easier to confide in a brother, than in an all-knowing, but all the more unknown Father. But can the Father know me, can I recognise him? I had a friend of the same age, one who understood everything. Now Titurel is inseparable from Piggy. Even during mass they put their heads together, neither of them is praying, and I see that the prayer book, at which they seem to be looking zealously, has a different print from ours. It will be a forbidden book, Casanova's *Memoirs* or Dumas' *Monte Cristo*, which they now devour with their eyes. It is bitter to have to watch, as Titurel, having finished reading a page sooner than the Prince, waits for the latter and as he does so fixes his eyes, with the eloquent expression I know so well, on the thick lips and the darting glances of the Prince's jam coloured eyes. So they profane God's hour. But am I any better? Where are my thoughts? Not with the Father, only with myself.

Admittedly on Saturday I did at last find a passage in the gospels which at least justifies my prayers and which should make it easier for me to entrust myself to God in the way that is required of a true Catholic. It is the continuation of the Sermon on the Mount in the Gospel According to St Matthew, chapter six. It begins well and with a fatherly voice (not of the Father in heaven, but of an earthly father – like a father who knows Onderkuhle and me): "But thou, when thou prayest, enter into thine inner chamber, and having shut thy door, pray to thy Father which is in secret, and thy Father which seeth in secret shall recompense thee . . . for your Father knoweth what things ye have need of, before ye ask him." It is followed in the gospel by the Lord's Prayer.

After supper, left alone by all, accompanied by polite greetings, I returned to my empty blueish-shadowy room. Then I kneel down like a pile of old clothes thrown on the floor, in which the cat often hides, in which it nestles and feels at home. But I do not have the strength to put an end to everything. I fall asleep in this unnatural position and awake in it at morning and go to my work, to give a swimming lesson in the Captain's stead. My lips still go on praying, as if even on the stairs, hurrying down to the breakfast room among the pupils, I hoped to comprehend the meaning of this prayer. Is it a prayer only for men? Is it one for those who labour with their hands? Is it for those who serve? Did my forebears not pray? The only thing that I understand are the words about our daily bread. It is not for me, that I must pray, but for my father. There is no word from him, no letter is lying on the breakfast table.

Is he in need? Troubled? He has no debts, not to a single person, rather they owe him a debt. Lead us not into temptation! I am so absorbed by my decisive battle between life and D., that nothing can lead me into temptation. Evil alone I understand, solely to be delivered from it would I have to pray, if I could believe.

Kingdom, Power, Glory, how much hope it would give me, if I could share in them, even if only in my thoughts. But I have nothing to hope for. One can achieve nothing great without hope, one cannot even subsist in mediocrity, if one sees everywhere the fingerprints of D. and cannot escape them. For ever! To stand up against the cosmos, to challenge infinity as a courageous aristocrat, I understand how redeeming that would be, liberating, pure happiness. But precisely because I know it and that I am struggling for it makes me weak instead of strong. I am afraid of D. I am going the wrong way like Cyrus in the green riding school. Why does no one catch me and guide me, better than I could guide myself?

2

On good days of exaltation, it is a particular pleasure of mine to jump from the highest springboard which is approximately seven metres above the swimming pool's surface. As straight as an arrow or with a supple curve in the dive. The main thing is to keep one's balance during the few seconds of the fall. To control oneself as one falls. The height is almost immaterial. Another skill is jumping with skis, which we cannot practise here, since in Onderkuhle snow is never sufficiently deep, nor is there a sufficiently steep slope. If the ski master from Norway succeeds in leaping from a ski-jump as tall as a house, then a good swimmer or diver can also without any risk plunge ten or even twenty metres and during these seconds experience all the pleasure of traversing empty space.

It cannot be very different to drop down in D., into the empty, fathomless space yawning before us or to rise into it, for that is the same.

But it is terrible, if someone such as I begins this jump in fear, if his legs fail him, if he sinks down like a piece of lead, like a rain-soaked, unfledged bird falling heavily from the branch despite its modest weight. The timid diver, however, arrives below to the accompaniment of maddening pain and receives a tremendous thrashing from the surface of the water. This must not happen. What courage cannot do, the will can. I clench my teeth, gather all my strength and dive straight as an arrow, my heart missing a beat, down to my comrades tumbling in the water below. They throw themselves on to their sides, on to their backs, swerve far away from me and exuberantly surround me with cheerful noise when I surface. They admire me respectfully, not knowing all my cowardice was needed, in order to summon up so much courage.

I know very well, that I did not succeed in the tests posed by the breaking of Cyrus and by the saving of Titurel's life, or if I did succeed, they were not decisive. But this little effort in a dive from a height of seven metres has given me some self-confidence again.

Yet how much closer to death is the Master with his grey hair, and yet he commands this as he does everything here. It is not he who is quickest at figures, but he holds the highest housekeeping post here in our little kingdom. He is assisted by the Bookkeeper, a retired but indestructible official, who has seven children to feed at home. He lives for them. Here he economises on everything, no matter how small the sum involved, even breaks the cigarettes he smokes in two before putting them between his lips, which look as if they are made of brown paper. I am not sure whether the roulette wheel which has been rotating for several days on the bed of a comrade in the "Fifth's" dormitory was smuggled in by him or by the Master. I would not put it past the Master to exploit the lower instincts of the pupils for gain, or equally the Bookkeeper to reap small extra profits, whether with or without the Master's consent. Money is something foreign to me. What has it go to do with Onderkuhle? What I yearn for, what I hunger for, cannot be bought for money, whether it is won by gaming or earned by labour.

Now that I can no longer regard Titurel as friend, I am often seen with Cyrus. I am thrilled by the presence of the big, grey horse, who recognises me and who stares at me unblinkingly with his strangely coloured eyes, which are very like those of the Master. His behaviour with me is odd. He bravely comes closer to me with the upper part of his body, but at the same time tries to flee with his haunches cowardly turned away from me. But I mean no harm. I know also, that I need hardly expect any harm from the animal who has been broken for ever. I saddle him myself, and in front of the stable door swing myself into the tight English saddle of pea-yellow, finely grained leather, grip reins and whip in my left hand. I start to trot, and to my great joy can soon feel how willingly the stallion obeys me, how attentively he complies with my directions, and how, no different from a first year pupil at his first lessons, he makes an effort to do everything correctly at my command. So I attempt easy jumping exercises over simple obstacles. The meadows have already been mown. It will soon be evening. I must not waste time. Smaller obstacles up to hay ricks the height of a man, the animal takes unhesitatingly. He just as easily jumps over quite wide ditches which have been dug for improvement purposes through a formerly swampy, now firm and fertile, grassy terrain. Then I am propelled towards the railway line from Onderkuhle to the small industrial town of V., which at one point runs through a deep cutting. This place too is a kind of ditch, not especially wide, but dangerous for the horse and, why keep silent about it, for me. I know it, and the horse knows it, if at all, only through me. For if the horse does not gain a footing on the escarpment, then we hurtle down on to the narrow iron rails below, and my spine is crushed between the track and the weight of the horse's body. True. But anyone who thinks like that will not jump. Anyone who turns away from the railway line at such a sharp angle is a coward. It is said.

Where to then? Above all back. Back across the low meadows of sulphur yellow lupins, giving out an intoxicatingly sweet perfume, on the back of an ever faster galloping horse, which now takes fright at a train entering the cutting below. He is spurred on to a furious speed, of which no one would have suspected him capable. Why should I deny that I too have always been afraid of machines and locomotives? This fear is not unfamiliar to small children, but to me, precocious beyond his years? Now I force myself to remain still and to force upon me and the horse at least the sight of the moving train. Hot milky steam pours out of the old-fashioned machine, which looks like a brass-bound teapot, and swirls in a swiftly fading cloud around the narrow dappled ankles of the horse in the meadow. It is still light. Lemon coloured butterflies of previously unseen shape waver in the air as if with four wings. One, almost transparent in its fluttering and weaving flight, looks as if roughly cut from yellow tissue paper. As I gallop, the sharp side of my uniform cap strikes it. It spirals downwards. Evidently it is badly injured. I dismount, in the impotence of my own cowardice and dazedness in the face of death, sympathising with all death. As soon as I touch the strange four-winged form with my rough riding gloves, I see that it is two butterflies. Their tapering bodies are welded to one another. They are half torn in pieces and yet do not leave off one another. A trace of life, impalpable mysterious will to exist, seems still to inhabit them. But more than that there is in them pain and certain extinction. The delicately jointed antennae pointing in different directions can be seen to vibrate. The eyes are glassy, yet grainy and quite immobile. Most affecting of all is a gentle, unfamiliar perfume which issues from these insects joined in death.

It does me good, and probably them also, if the heel of my boot crushes them. So it buries them in the bloom of youth in the middle of the deep-breathing, perfume-filled meadow. So I experience pity to a degree of which I have never before been conscious. For why does a man need to feel pity, as long as he stands in the middle of the intoxication of life? Only when life is drawing to a close, when he has to avert his gaze from the stronger sun, does he understand pity and no longer resists it.

The courage to face life on bad days – that is magnificent. It is magnificent to bravely plunge into danger and triumph over death like the fire cat. It is magnificent if someone knows no danger, is without doubts. If he breathes with such a complete satisfaction of all lust for life, that even the air, the drizzling rain intoxicates him, if racing on the back of a horse spurs him on to forget himself entirely! How different now my own timid trotting on the tall nag, through the transparent, flickering evening filled with chirping and coupling insects, where I shiver in the warm air. Where alone and having fallen out with myself, I turn my eyes shyly away from the setting sun, although its flames long ago lost their greatest, most dangerous strength. I allow my ghostly, slim, elongated shadow to glide across the lush carpet of grass in front of me, as if I could thereby avoid breaking a single blade of grass. I live without making a sound, cowardly, fading with each moment, trembling before the next, because I sense the last one. Where is the other Orlamünde?

I turn my horse homewards, the horse longs for the stable and so braces his muscles in a spontaneous, very fast gallop showing a furious joy in the race. But where am I? On the vast, almost metallically green meadow before my eyes, part of a city has sprung up. I see a fairly high, but discoloured and in places already crumbling, vermilion factory wall. The wall is pierced by small dark windows, which look like hatches, but are oddly arranged. Beside them a kind of gateway, where something is moving now, an overturned motor lorry with its wheels in the air, and behind that, already almost dissolving into the clouds on the horizon, a rectangular, grey stone factory chimney, to which, at ground level, however, a newer section made of brighter red bricks has been added. How did all this find its way here, within the boundaries of Onderkuhle College, in the meadowland south of the school, where a factory never existed? I would like to look at it more closely. But the closer I ride the more the mirage dissolves, and if I want to return to the earlier position, then my horse bridles, whets its teeth impatiently against the bit, looks up at me from the side and pricks up his ears. What should I do? Chase after the curious natural phenomenon and thereby put the fruits of breaking in the horse at risk or timidly submit? Do I submit?

3

_____

With Duke Ondermark, who is member of the board of trustees of our institution, is expected his secretary, who is to undertake an audit of our finances. Consequently the Bookkeeper, the "indestructible official", is constantly on the go. We feel sorry for him, and Prince Piggy, who otherwise never lends his motorbike (which he, by the way, almost never uses) to anyone, has yielded it to the Bookkeeper for a few days, in case he should need it for journeys to V., where most of the suppliers to Onderkuhle College are to be found. We know that the Bookkeeper has to provide for a family of eight. He therefore not only goes short himself, but sees his children go short too, the youngest especially, whom he cannot even comfort by his presence. For duty keeps him here throughout the year, just like the Master and myself, whereas the others, the Headmaster, Abbé, teachers and tutors, even the lesser officials and craftsmen right down to the servants are entitled, just like the pupils, to leave. But the Bookkeeper and I are not the same. Whereas I was able to bask in the Master's favour, the Bookkeeper remains for ever in his shadow. He is not so much the Master's right hand as the sole of his shoe, on which the Master steps as if it were the most natural thing in the world. Though the relationship of the gaunt, dried up Bookkeeper to us is neither one of comradeship nor of authority, we nevertheless greet him, and some of the generous lads bring him toys for his children. Now, despite the heat, we see him squeezed into his long, greasy shiny coat; from early morning until late evening he runs back and forward between his office and the store rooms and store houses, rattles off to town on the motorbike, comes back clothed in grey dust, unloads the dirt-covered briefcases and immediately, even as his little eyes search for the Master, he puts one of the broken-in-half two centime cigarettes of black Algerian tobacco between his lips. Despite these exertions his lips are pale and even now while smoking cannot interrupt the mechanical motion of counting and calculating, so that frequently a stub falls to the ground where it is pecked up and plucked to pieces by one of the hens which are always cackling greedily around the yard. Piggy, of course, cannot restrain his barking laugh, but the rest of us throw the Bookkeeper new cigarettes, which he, "for safety's sake", jams between the pages of the big account book, before, with the heavy briefcases under his thin clerk's arms, shiny head stretching forward, he disappears like a lizard through the dark door of his office.

I surprise him then at times, when the yard has been abandoned by the pupils, in excited conversation with the Master; they throw figures and incomprehensible business expressions at one another, but both fall silent when they catch sight of me. I go away and reflect, not without bitterness, that here a most good-natured, modest family man is continually being kept from his family without him being able to free it from the most pressing cares. He pursues every kind of business, postponing repayment of loans, arranging discounts, but neglects his own business. We, however, the sons without fathers? Can the Master, despite his perhaps

genuine affection, replace my father? Now he has left the
Bookkeeper alone, no matter how unwillingly the latter lets
him go and hurries after me. I only walk all the more quickly.

I have not explained it before now, but it has to be said,
that I hate to be touched by another's hand. It is an inherited
peculiarity of my family on my mother's side. I have
described my mother as she is, as the most child-like,
coquettish, delightful person there is. But have I said that
my mother always shrank from me? She played with everything. She put her hand into the mouth of an always sickly
dog, now long dead, without fear, but me she touched only
with the greatest reluctance. This was the only cause of the
discord between my father and her. She never laid a hand
on me, either out of tenderness or to punish me. And I
inherit this from her, hardly ever draw close to her mouth,
her hand or her neck, which she likes to adorn with pearls,
other than for a kiss breathed more than actually placed with
warm lips. It is incomprehensible, shocking and yet at once
reassuring to me, when my old master roughly presses me
to his badly shaven cheeks and when he tries to kiss me on
the mouth with his drooping, tired, dull red lower lip, which
I, however, fend off so skilfully, that he does not notice my
aversion. Or is he merely too refined to reveal it to me?

Now the Master follows me in the yard in front of the
infirmary and takes my hand, in which I still carry the torn
scraps of an uncompleted letter to my parents. I would not
give my father, the noblest of men, my hand as I do now
the Bondsman, without a tormenting feeling of anguish. But
I submit to the Master in everything. It is both shocking
and reassuring, how with this contact the presentiment of
D., which has been pursuing me all day and did not even
leave me the peace of mind to write the letter to my father,
how this D. now immediately disappears, when the Master

takes my hand in his. Is it imprisonment? Tenderness? Is he my master? Am I the servant?

Finally the pull of my hand must tell him, that I wish to take my leave. Without looking at me he lets me go. Why has my hand become so weak that it lets fall the scraps of paper, the useless ruins of a never written confession, which are caught by the hot, sandy wind, wild in its heat, and now begin a flight which takes them past the closed windows of the college, almost to the roof of the red school building glaring in the heat?

4

The time of the great thunderstorms, whose downpours had all night long filled the dormitories with balmy scent, is over. It has been followed by cloudless weather, unusually hot for the end of June. A stormy wind always seems to be swooping from the milky white or yellow haze at the edge of the horizon, its strength but not its direction always remaining constant. The schoolboys' eyes redden because of the dust, which is carried to us from far away, we leave the building as little as possible and at night frequently even have to shut the windows, since the blustering wind allows no one any peace. Whoever, like me, lives in the upper storey of the pupils' wing, can often not get a wink of sleep during the early hours of the night, no matter how much he longs to do so, since the very hot roof tiles radiate a terrible heat. The beams which have gradually dried out completely begin to creak, only then to contract with a groan in the cooler morning hours, so that neither in the hour around midnight nor in those of morning twilight does one get the rest which is needed in this unnatural period of time above all. As a consequence of this "unnatural" period a bad harvest cannot be ruled out, and the Bookkeeper, who wanted to sell part of the crop in V., returns on the motorbike with a quite desperate, all the paler face. Or is something else the cause of his despair? What is so important about a few bushels? Beside the outwardly calm Master his agitation appears almost comical. Who indeed would want to stifle his laughter, when the indestructible official, the careworn Bookkeeper, wrapped in his doleful thoughts, swallows the remainder of his unlit cigarette? But this laughter does not come from my heart. How gladly I would like to help him! Perhaps he only needs a small sum to balance his mismanaged accounts? But among the poorest and most needy pupils of Onderkuhle none is poorer than I, none more needy; even if I do not see only lack of money as poverty, nor succour in a few thousand francs, as does this poor father of seven in his threadbare grey-black suit . . .

Now comes the last night in Onderkuhle or the last night of Onderkuhle. For that is the same. I have outlasted Onderkuhle. It is no more. Indeed: what remained of me after the fire of Onderkuhle is only called Boëtius von Orlamünde, but is another being. Or does it only seem to me to be so?

After the communal supper (how well I still remember today the cherries which were served for dessert, dark red, wet from the water in which they had been rinsed, and on the stalks remnants of leaves, which had, however, been burnt almost to tinder by the immoderate sun), after supper I go to my little room which, with its many superfluous writing tables, seems to me doubly empty and inhospitable, since Titurel no longer sets foot in it. His behaviour to me is no more than that of a well-mannered comrade, I no longer appear in his "duties and accounts", not in his hate, still less in his love. He has extinguished me, or, worse still, for him, my existence has extinguished itself of its own accord, so that I do not even provoke him to anger nor even to contradiction – for this at least would be a sign to me, that I still exist for him. It is over.

I then take a cold shower and retire to bed. The coolness brought from the shadowy bathroom does me good. Objects remain benevolent, they never refuse their loyalty . . . I fall fast asleep immediately.

Only a quarter of an hour later, however, I awake. Outside my window, which faces south and despite the eerie moaning wind is wide open, the clear, starry, ultramarine sky stretches to the wooded hills of the furthest horizon. I know many of the stars from my school lessons. The geography of the earth was also always a favourite subject, I can quite vividly imagine the earth with its continents and vast oceans and yet at the same time keep in view its shape as a globe, always call cities, mountain ranges and rivers in their immovable locations to mind, which in this respect never lets me down. But I was aroused even more by the boundless spherical geography of the eternally moving, rotating firmament, the names and positions, spectral colours and classes of the stars, about which I was always asking our old teacher (a retired naval officer). Until now the sight of them was as beneficial for me as for most people. One cannot always remain amid the confusion of mankind. One cannot live easily with one's own unsatisfied and unrealisable desires. Without a friend, the longing for father and home cannot always be vanquished by sport and work. Man too gladly flees the unrest of his own heart to gaze at the stars and is refreshed, comforted by their harmony, by their gentle, noiseless progress. So had I been until this night. But no description can convey the panic terror which grips me tonight at the sudden appearance of the brightly glittering stars. In particular one constellation, in the lower half of the sky, consisting of five stars, fills me with horror, and of the five it is again one in particular, standing highest in the sky and which is said to be one million years distant from us, by which I remain transfixed. What sense is there in fear? Fear is meaningless. A small, nameless being, destined for a lifespan of at most sixty to seventy years, and even within this short span always wavering between life and death, needs to fear nothing less than these heavenly bodies, which never know us, never notice us, are for ever alien to us. What are we to them? Nothing, less than nothing. We do not exist for them. What are they to us? Only a beautiful sight, something that arouses nobler feelings, like the blue flags of our aristocratic college, emblems without substance and reality. So speaks reason. But it is never convincing. To escape the dread I futilely let fall the coarse linen curtains, causing the iron rod round which they are rolled to hurtle down onto the window-sill with a dull sound like a severed head. Yet the terrible brilliance of the stars breaks through. They dazzle, and the one particular star of the five shines especially brightly through the fine gaps in the worn fabric. In vain do I wrap myself around me as in a blanket, I remember my singular red-haired existence. I think of my achievements, of my "accounts and duties", of my goals in life, of geography and history, sport and horses, I attempt in vain, to draft a letter to my father, to him, whom I miss so much, especially now! Only a line from him, a letter, like those of which I had already received so many without great thanks and even without deep emotion – and everything would be different. The thought of the infinite reaches ever more deeply into me. Something palpably twists inside me and suddenly I hear myself sigh and groan, as the horse Cyrus, conquered by inner pressure, groaned. Must it not have been terrible to hear me sighing or groaning, if the attention of the boys in the dormitory next door is drawn? Their roulette wheel stops whirring round, some stand up and come to the door, to ask after me and despite my silence by repeated knocking and even whistling to invite me to join them. For all the sympathy there is also mockery, I know it. It shows greater pride to remain alone.

I am still struggling with all my force against the terrible in itself, against being smashed to pieces. A small child, who in warmer lands is laid beneath the night-time constellations, which there perhaps gleam even more brightly, bears this sight without further ado, he smiles, licks the last drops of milk from his thick Piggy lips and falls asleep. But I, an Orlamünde? Should I flee before it? I must? Play roulette with the others, when things have turned serious here? *Whom* can I then meet without fear? Against what can I prevail? What is to become of me? But I feel it, if I deliberately turn my head and still the poisonous rays of the fifth star enter my eyes through the gaps in the old curtain – I am only stubborn like the horse Cyrus, no longer brave. Once I dreamt of a death under this horse, now I see a death, just as it awaits this horse, before me.

To judge by the position of the stars, it must be close to midnight. The heat is hardly to be borne any more. I can no longer bear myself. So I go to my comrades, who receive me as if I had only just left their company. They are almost all still awake, sit upright, some half clothed, some naked because of the heat. Titurel wears pyjamas, which he has grown out of, which I already knew when they were still too big for him. He sets the roulette wheel spinning with his big tanned yellow hand, while Piggy watches him with his cherry jam coloured eyes and yet his eyes also do not stray from the sums which the pupils are staking. Since I have no money and do not want to play without a stake, I am given the office of operating the wheel. It has a spring, which is wound up as far as possible and then let go with a whirr. The arrow then stops at changing positions, indicates number and colour. So it goes on for hours. Some pupils have ready money, gold and silver coins, others write figures on scraps of paper from their notebooks, there are also a few who give and take articles of value in place of money. Piggy watches over everything like that, whereas Titurel devotes himself entirely to the game as such. Meanwhile morning is breaking. A smoky dulling of the clear ultramarine sky has appeared at the edge of the horizon. A few have already been over-powered by tiredness; they have dozed off, lie on their sides, the ribs of their naked torsos rise and fall, one holds a slowly burning cigarette between his pale, full lips, on which the first down of a moustache casts its shadow, until another, younger boy pulls it away laughing, others have rolled up like hedgehogs and are snoring loudly, still holding the notes of stakes and winnings in their hands. One boy gathers up the liqueur bottles by their necks and hides them in a drawer of the big college cupboard. The cocks can be heard crowing outside. There is a fluttering in the bushes, and the songbirds begin the first, almost inaudible, very sweet flute notes, which are intentionally very long drawn out, as if they were questions. They flit through the damp air of the already dove-grey dawn, still uncertain they rise up in the morning mist and sink down, letting themselves fall quickly like small weights. The smoky strip on the horizon has changed into a white shaggy fleece and filled with blood. The undersides of elongated clouds begin to shine like oranges. All of a sudden it is quite light and the red has become a pulsing glow, which the naked eye can hardly bear. The boys have all fallen asleep, no one pays attention to the roulette wheel except Piggy, who watches tirelessly and keeps all the remaining stakes. Afterwards he removes the roulette wheel as his property.

I return to my room, which, in contrast to the stale air of the dormitory which smells of cigarettes, is filled by a fragrant aroma of sage, blown across from the freshly mown meadows by the cooler morning wind. Now the estate workers leave their houses in small groups. The Master appears shivering and pale in front of the school and looks round. Then he quickly goes into the main building, presumably to dust the blue flags before his first round of inspection. A baker arrives with a large basket full of bread. The room is filled by the light of the magnificently rising sun, the restlessness of the horses in the stables can be heard, the lowing of the hungry cattle and soft and familiar the scratching and questioning mewing of my fire cat, which during the night has been roving the meadows and fields, where it went to hunt mice. Now it fawns its way in, wants to rub up against me with its still blood-spattered mouth, arching its fire red back and purring. Now it wants to curl up at my feet on the college blanket and sleep. For a long time it looks for the most comfortable position, while the purring grows louder. The very poorly constructed college bed trembles too – to the accompaniment of this sound I at last fall asleep.

5

There must have been something of the Onderkuhle fire in that night's dream. Admittedly it is not clear to me how it could be possible for Onderkuhle to burn twice over, and for the first time during my brief sleep, between four and eight in the morning, disturbed by gusts of wind, and then in reality on the evening of that day. I know only, that I am woken by the pupils returning to the dormitory at an unwonted hour to put on their gala uniforms. The Duke has just telegraphed the Headmaster from the large railway station closest to Onderkuhle that he, together with his secretary, prefers to be fetched by carriage, rather than continue the journey by the branchline. I overhear this from the lads' conversations and for myself act accordingly. By chance I look out and see the Master standing beside the "indestructible official" in the buzzing morning heat, but they are not talking to one another, only their hands move restlessly, finally the Master pulls himself together and walks back towards his lodging; the Bookkeeper follows him as if hypnotised, so lost in thought that he is almost run down by the carriage, drawn by our best horses, which is just setting off. I am the third person sunk in dreams, who knows that he has dreamed something significant but has not yet properly made sense of this vision.

In a very short time the carriage appears again. In the back sits a simply dressed man of approximately forty-five years of age. He is wearing a very loose but superbly cut English travelling suit. He is small rather than tall and does not have a military bearing. Only when he is speaking do his already somewhat slack features become taut. The unconscious, the inborn ability to command (a rare talent) becomes obvious when he refuses something: then he holds his left forearm bent at a right angle, pushing what he does not wish into depths visible only to him, so that it is never mentioned again. By contrast, when he wants to have something, he simply beckons what is desired with the index finger of his right hand, at the same time slightly raising the yellowish, long and very narrow skull, covered with short hair. He is evidently giving the secretary sitting beside him all kinds of reminders and instructions relating to the organisation of the whole day. The Duke must leave again in the evening, at about ten, a special train is waiting for him, since he must attend an important meeting in Brussels the next morning. With a great effort of will the Duke tries to overcome his somewhat morose and mistrustful character, as well as to conceal the signs of deafness, which is probably caused by the powerful ear drum shattering Winchester rifles, such as have to be employed on hunts in the tropics. He has on many occasions been on such hunts in the Congo and the English Sudan. He beckons the Headmaster, sweating in his gold embroidered suit, over to his right side, evidently because he can hear better on it, then, as he regards the Colonel's lips with a displeased expression, forbids all titles and high-flown speeches and insists on simplicity. His face brightens when he catches sight of us, neatly drawn up in our new uniforms, but it is our persons and not the gala uniforms or the parade order which cheer him, for he gathers us around him on the spot and requests us to put on our ordinary uniforms. In other respects too this day is to be in no way different from an ordinary schoolday in Onderkuhle, such as those he knew here in his youth.

With a great cheer we now discard the special uniforms. It is a cry which is completely against the rules. But the Master, who stands in the background and takes in everything with his ice-grey eyes, smiles at it. He rarely smiles, and his smile that day decided a great deal for me. After the outbreak of the fire the suspicion arose that the Master, whose "irregularities" everyone here knew about, but no one dared criticise, had laid the fire of Onderkuhle together with the Bookkeeper, who was mixed up in various rackets (interest and extension of credit, stock exchange speculation and losses at the college's expense) and who had cause to fear investigation by the Duke's secretary. Although appearances suggested it, I do not believe it. I do not believe that the Master is guilty. Firstly because indeed all the Master's worldly goods, his hard, and in some measure honestly won property, were destroyed in the fire, but above all because of the benevolent, gentle, paternal smile, with which he watched the young people, whooping, cheering and already undressing in the yard and on the stairs.

But why speak of the conflagration already? The walls of the tall, red, castle-like building still stand, the grey linen twill curtains still flap at the windows. At this moment the horses and cattle, in so far as they are not to be found in the meadow, still live safe and sound in the usual stalls, and of the whole fire there is as yet nothing save for a premonition in the heart of eighteen-year-old Boëtius von Orlamünde. With the other boys I now enter the oppressively sultry dormitory of the "Fifth", filled with glittering brightness, glance into the quickly opened, huge cupboards, where the uniforms and other belongings of the pupils are to be found in separate numbered drawers. Only then do I start, for I have long been banished from this room, I realise my mistake and go back to my closet. Titurel, half unclothed while undressing, gives me a strangely cold look. Prince Piggy merely puts his head to one side so that proper folds of fat form at his sturdy, yellowish neck. In my room I see the fire cat, which is still fast asleep and has made itself a small hollow in my bed. A minute later I hurry to the swimming lesson in the hall, where I am to deputise for the riding master who is away.

The Duke has meanwhile left behind his secretary, who is to set to work with the Bookkeeper on the books and cash audit. The Duke himself wishes to be with the youngest class, which is now receiving its first swimming lesson. The majority can, however, already swim when they enter the establishment, only a few, the most timid, cannot do so. There is a blond, very pretty boy, ten years old, as old as I was when I came here. He is a little afraid of the water. It is noticeable as soon as he comes out of the cabin. The green and white striped swimming costume is too large for him. The boy shivers. He cannot be shivering with cold on this buzzing, very hot June day. But he pulls himself together, pushes his thin neck forward, looks bravely at me, the water and the Duke. At home his affectionate mother has let his silken ash blond hair grow down over his low, girlish forehead, at whose lower border the equally ash blond eyebrows are drawn as if with a very fine crayon. He speaks in a bright silvery voice, he defends himself under his breath without surrendering his pride, without admitting his weakness, against the good-natured or even malicious jokes of his comrades, who are making fun of him, because he is to be on the "fishing rod", on which, however, almost all of them also once were, for how else should one learn to swim?

Admittedly there are also people, whom one can simply throw into the water or who throw themselves into the water (like myself) and swim immediately, badly it is true and with a great waste of effort – but they do it. They are rare. I myself ensure that the straps of the fishing rod are properly buckled on. The fishing rod is the apparatus used in all swimming establishments. It consists of a pole, which the swimming master pulls and the straps belonging to it, which are put around the pupil. I wait until the agitation of the boy, whom we have called Alma Venus or simply Alma, has died down somewhat, until his delicate skin feels cool to the touch and his pulse is beating calmly. But precisely this care seems to weigh on Alma, for his girlish brow grows ever redder, his pretty lips twitch, his slender body stretches ever more clumsily, and entire rivers of sweat trickle under the two straps at his chest. So: into the water as quickly as possible – and all will be well.

Then the Duke, who knows my father well, steps up to me. He offers me his hand, which I take respectfully, he leans over the brass railing of the swimming pool beside me and passes on greetings to my father. He notices, however, that at this moment my attention is divided. He gives me a friendly wave of his strong, yellow, manly hand, which is adorned with no ring, but only with a broad scar, which has turned dark brown. I turn again to my Alma. The few moments of waiting have, however, severely undermined the boy's moral power of resistance. Now his beautiful lips tighten. The teasing of his comrades, who do not feel in the least put out by the presence of a member of the royal house, causes him alternately to turn pale and flush, his first tears, fortunately observed only by me, fall into the water of the swimming pool, stirred up into small waves by the pupils. Under other circumstances I would have postponed the swimming lesson until we, Alma and I, were alone.

Now, however, the Duke's attention has been drawn. He is distantly related to Alma. He leans against the railing in his light English travelling suit (pepper and salt) and whispers to the boy on the fishing rod, "Take heart, child! Off you go!" But this only makes the poor boy take fright completely. He now weeps quite openly, while carrying out the pre-scribed movements, as I have taught them to him at the preparatory lesson on the mattress, in an entirely mechanical manner. And after a few feeble strokes the unbelievable hap-pens: Alma loses his head, begins to cry for his mother and to clasp with both hands the iron rail which runs along the side of the whole pool, level with the surface of the water. Naturally I pay no attention – notice only that I am turning red. Even in the greatest danger I would never have thought of my mother. I would never have called her. Only my father. Only a father has the strength to stand beside me and help me in my fear of D. – but how far away is he now? I have had no news from him for five weeks now. But I control myself – I also tell the pitiable Alma's shrieking and maliciously yelling comrades to be quiet. I continue to com-mand. I walk forward step by step with my rod and drag the helplessly failing Alma along with me. I am, of course, stronger than he. He must follow. He must let go of the iron rail. Nothing can happen to him. Admittedly the pool is so deep here, that a piece of lead could sink down or a man drowning on purpose could go under, but after all the boy has me to protect him from death.

The Duke has observed this example of fear of water very disapprovingly. In vain do the Headmaster and one of the tutors try to draw him away from the scene of failure of one of the pupils of our college. The Duke, however, remains here as if rooted to the spot, precisely for that reason, and devotes to this incident, familiar to every swimming teacher, an attention which it certainly does not deserve. "Just give it to me!" he says and takes the swimming rod out of my hand. By abruptly raising the instrument he causes the boy to rise out of the water just like a fish caught on a line. Then he, the Duke, pushes the rod further out, so that the lad can no longer catch hold of the railing. Then the Duke lowers the rod so much that the linking rope becomes slack and Alma's torso is completely submerged in the water. "Come on!" calls the Duke in a low voice. "Off you go! You should be ashamed of yourself"

However, the boy hears nothing any more. Helplessly the unfortunate thrashes about with arms and legs and with his pretty little head. The hair, gold blond, glinting in the water like fish scales, falls into his face, almost into his eyes. He splutters and cries, "Help, mother! I'm drowning!" Loud laughter from the pupils. I am ashamed for him. The Duke turns dark red. He throws the pole to the boy as if he is weary of the whole business. But now the whole length of it rocks in the pool. The boy is no longer suspended from it. Now he really does sink down in the water. No one seems to notice. His comrades only laugh and splash one another and him with the lukewarm water. The Duke has turned aside and is conversing with the teachers, who are joined by Piggy.

As a consequence of movements at once strenuous and restricted, Alma has turned over in the water, he is lying on his side, gurgling he calls for help.

His situation is not without danger, as his left leg has become entangled in the rope. I have no choice but to dive headfirst into the water and grab hold of the pole. At the smacking sound (the improvised dive has not been faultless) the Duke turned round astonished. Now he roars with laughter. I drag Alma, who has turned blue, out of the water. He is trembling and appears to be unconscious. I now have a strong feeling of pity. That should not be. It is inconsistent with the spartan and unnatural philosophy of life at Onderkuhle. So the poor little boy, the moral infant, is treated like a leper. He is ordered to be confined, is not allowed to be present at the midday meal. That is the punishment for his cowardice, for his fear of D. The fencing room is designated as the place of punishment. I help the bewildered boy to dress as a father helps his son. I take him up to the fencing room, which smells of rusty rapiers and carbolic acid. Afflicted by cowardice myself, and with the terrible dream of the nocturnal blaze in my heart, I would like to do something good for the poor little coward, perhaps give him the possibility of spending his confinement in the dormitory next door and sleeping away the black day. I resist this stirring of cowardly leniency and unmanly tenderness and lead Alma, who is quietly but unmistakably reluctant, to the bench against the wall of the fencing loft and from the outside scrupulously lock him into the overheated room, which is directly under the roof. The rest of us sit down to table under the blue flags in the big cadet mess and, noisy as sparrows, eat dinner with boisterous gaiety. Good wine and liqueurs, unaccustomed pleasures, make their contribution.

After the very sumptuous meal, we all proceed to the park. Smoking, otherwise only tolerated as a secret but unavoidable vice, is permitted by the Colonel, the Headmaster himself, on this festive day, only he asks us to be careful with the matches, for the heat of recent days, together with the hot wind, blowing today also, which fills the whole countryside with a hissing sound, has parched everything, from the roof shingles to the leaves falling early from the trees. If a glowing matchstick falls to the ground, then the grass, very dry and rustling like paper, flares up into flame within three seconds, until one stamps out the little fire under the soles of one's shoes.

We have assembled around the Duke, as if we were all one family, like the royal family, listen to his reports, to which he treats us in quite a sober form, for example by recalling his hunts for wild buffalo and white rhinoceros with complete precision as to time and place, while simply summing up other hunting expeditions, e.g. in the English Sudan, to the effect that there one can shoot everything from man to the bird of paradise. If a school like ours is the proper one, if the teaching of the arts of riding, swimming, fencing is true, if the cultivation of manly qualities, courage, bearing and form, disregard for one's life to the point of contempt for death is the proper goal of existence, then an existence such as the Duke leads, consisting of hunting, travelling and perilous geographical discoveries, must be the absolute quintessence of life. So I feel it to be.

Close to the Duke, and perhaps not recognisable to everyone, there is a smell of Russia leather or hippopotamus whip; a smell half pungent, half sweet, which I inhale with particular pleasure. The sight of the Duke is a help for me, an important and indispensable one, especially on this day, I confess it.

The Duke is very fond of me. Admittedly he only favours me with a glance or with a minute inclination of his body, by slightly raising his voice when he speaks to me. My father and he were comrades here. But how much has their existence altered since then! But no time to think of that now. If he, my father, has hidden from all the world the princely distress of his family, then I too can be silent. To the world my father is still the great man. He is present at every exclusive reception, which he attends in a black dress suit, wearing as only decoration an Austrian order, perhaps the highest, a knight commander's star, which apart from him, is conferred only on crowned heads. But is our lineage of Orlamünde not just as ancient, just as good as that of the Habsburgs? The Duke's suit is quite plain and without any mark of distinction. This man belongs to a new age. This man, a different kind of pupil of our school, loves no pomp, his uniform is the English travelling suit, pepper-and-salt. His order is the broad scar on his right hand. Like all of us, he too lives only among men, the comrades of his travels, bearers of his rifle, drivers of his pack-animals, which he requires on his expeditions. He will not often be seen at court. His court is the Royal Geographical Society, where he sits among professors as if among his equals, listens carefully, since his hearing has been impaired, and where he does not scorn dark tinted glasses of which he, whose eyes have been weakened by the tropical sun, avails himself now too, in the glittering light of the afternoon sun.

Everything on this endless, fiery golden, transparent summer day gives me pleasure. I clutch at the courage, the superiority, the stoicism of the Duke. The previous night lies far behind me. It is almost completely gone, together with its dreams of conflagration. The world, "on the whole benevolent", comparatively secure, calms me now, especially near the Duke, and in his presence, surrounded by the Russia leather-like smell and cigar smoke, resting on a deck chair as he is, with a view of the park and the school buildings, I long for trials, to calmly prove myself in them and at last to redeem myself completely.

6

_____

My whole existence would be changed if I could live at the side of a man such as the Duke. He is stronger, cleverer, more resolute than I. He seems to be able to read my eyes, he looks at me for a long time with his pale blue, brightly sparkling eyes, which actually seem to be looking at something situated behind me, yet at the same time go to the heart of me. I have never found it possible to talk about what concerns me. I have always admitted my wishes only to myself. I have never missed my mother here. But I have always felt the absence of my father and never more so than at this moment. "I was here with your father thirty years ago. It may be that I had suggested he join me on the First Expedition. At that time he already knew your charming lady mother . . ." He gave no further reason for my father rejecting the offer, he does not say that he regrets that my father has chosen the career of a "prince without a position". "We always have too few people with us and too many. We could make good use of a sportsman in top condition, someone who has studied medicine, animal diseases too, can shoot and prepare animal hides, possesses an ability to find his bearings and a degree of scientific curiosity and who leaves Europe for a few years with a light heart. Besides that, a knowledge of languages is also indispensable. English for everyday use. One has to be able to absorb the languages of the natives from one day to the next and not forget them quickly. And yet there are districts in Central Africa, where each village speaks its own language. These languages are dying out, but how much can be saved! Once an explorer came back with a wagon load of ivory tusks and lion skins and 5,600 plant species, today with such and such a number of dying languages and cultures, fetishes, primitive art, myths and customs. I see you, Orlamünde, I can easily imagine your behaviour on an expedition. Apart from you, I could only take a liking to Prince X., the one whom you all call Piggy . . ."

At this moment the secretary steps up to the Duke, to ask if he has any further instructions. At the very same second we hear a window-pane burst in that part of the college where the offices are accommodated and from where the secretary has just come. First of all, I think that one of the pupils, Piggy perhaps, whose unmistakable barking laugh can be heard, might have smashed a window out of high spirits. But then alarmed shouts can be heard. Suddenly there is dead silence, everyone has left us. Everyone is clustered round the administration office, from whose broken window we, the Duke, his secretary and I, can from far off already see dull blue, transparent cigarette smoke-like wisps escaping. The Master, white as the wall of the administration building, runs past us, calls, "It's burning", and hurries through the park to the farm buildings, to open up the fire-houses to which he has the keys. We quickly approach the scene of the fire. The smoke has become thicker, it hangs in front of the door like tissue paper. Inside the house there is a humming like in a beehive.

Helpless, the people, boys and adults, stand together in

front of the entrance. The smoke pours out ever more thickly, admixed with something especially pungent, heavy. The hissing of the fire can be heard. Suddenly a suppressed groan (it is not for the first time that I hear this groan, which is like a saw being drawn through freshly cut wood) comes out of the burning interior. I do not stop to think for a moment. I pull the brim of my cap lower into my face, put on my old Swedish riding gloves, walk forward, grasp the hot door handle and plunge into the office.

I immediately take everything in. The fire started from the motorcycle, which has no business being in the Bookkeeper's office, and on which the petrol tank, mounted on the frame between the wheels, must just have been opened. But the fuel has not yet properly flowed out, and that is why the petrol is burning so gently, it is now spreading, popping a little, over the floor and walls, which are covered with shelves. Enormous quantities of old, somewhat damp paper must be collected here. A heavy iron safe, untouched, stands in the corner like a little tower of lead. Worst of all is the thick grey-blue smoke pouring from the glowing, worthless paper. In the corner to the right of the window, which still remains untouched by the fire, leans or crouches a man; only now do I see him clearly, he sits there cross-legged, his pointed knees sticking out, and breathes in the smoke, as if it was coming from a broken-in-half cigarette, which he holds unlit in his faded lips: the Bookkeeper. His greasy black clothes shine in the light of the flames. I understand everything. I reach for him, seize him by the collar, as one seizes a horse by the halter, and pull him out of the corner towards the door. He resists fearfully, he holds his thin clerk's hands protectively over his yellow, gleaming head, when I use force he clings to one of the familiar high desks, whose legs are already beginning to glow. He has spent years at them, writing and counting, and now wants to die with them. No one but he can have started the fire. First he stares and says nothing, then he opens his mouth like a yawning cat, tears flow from his small black eyes, and he collapses. He does not want to leave. He writhes on the floor, clasps my knees, calls me by the names of his children: Paul, Jeanne, Chéri. The fire is already humming more loudly. Silently it has taken possession of the desks and shelves. The Book-keeper's arson is a kind of suicide. Is it worth saving such a creature? But it must be. The pneumatic tyres of the motor-cycle smoulder and give off overpowering fumes, then they burst simultaneously and become glittering hoops. Now, while I overpower the frail criminal by force, flames lick at the petrol tank. With one hand I draw his loosened necktie into a knot, with the other I hold his back, make him shuffle in front of me. Even at the door he bends down for a piece of paper, the fragment of a bill, which the Duke's secretary has checked and signed. So clouded (or so clear?) is the arsonist's mind that at such a moment he bends down for a scrap of paper, worthless to all and to him. Yet it is high time, for hardly are we out of the building, than with a dull explosion all the window-panes of the front burst and suddenly the previous buzzing murmur of the flames is trans-formed into a rapid, rhythmical metallic crackling. I never knew that fire can produce a sound like that of steel castanets. Now for the first time I see actual flames leap from the accounts room. The hot wind above the crowns of the trees has risen still further, as it has done every evening for weeks. Should nature make an exception, to save beloved Onder-kuhle? There is indescribable confusion everywhere. The cows in the byres, which have returned especially early from the meadow today because of the heat, kick against the walls and fodder racks in their fear, rattle the chains by which they

are secured. The hens flap up, drop down clumsily and
awkwardly again, while the doves circle high above their
cotes, their grey is gilded by the glare of the fire or by the
slowly sinking sun. Who can distinguish which? Who stares
at the sky, as if he could snatch something from there, which
undoes everything? I do not believe in God's aid. I believe
that it is necessary to hurry to the stables where the horses
are. I breathe a little life into the staring stable-boys who are
grinning stupidly with fear. What is required is quickly done.
Our leaders are completely incompetent. The old Abbé,
usually so brave, kneels on the chapel steps quickly and
mechanically saying the rosary, the Headmaster and the
teachers, surrounded by the tutors, "give orders", want to
systematically isolate and fight the fire, but they do not see
that it is spreading irresistibly from the "isolated" administration building, and the profound emotion of the alcoholic
Headmaster, which expresses itself in large tears, appears
repellent and ridiculous. The Master is sorely missed. He
mounted the first horse he found and rode to the railway
station, in order from there to alert the fire brigade of the
nearest town by telegraph. Our conservative boys' college
has never had a telephone line. It was not wanted. The Duke
is calm, dominating, in full possession of his faculties. He
has assembled the pupils around him. They take over the
old-fashioned pump from the servants. It is rolled up as
quickly as possible. The hoses are laid out, connected to the
hydrants, and the first thin jet of water is directed against
the red school building, glowing with heat, but still
untouched by the fire, in which are to be found the big
classrooms, the cadets' mess and the dormitories of the
Fourth and the Fifth. The Headmaster is a nuisance. He
runs about, wringing his hands, followed by his satellites.
He would prefer to remove the boys entrusted to him from

the vicinity of the burning administration building immediately. The Duke, however, does not permit it. Meanwhile the fire has spread swiftly. I go back and forward in the greatest haste. The stable-boys cannot master the horses. I first of all tie an elderly grey mare to a tree in the orchard. Now I attend to Cyrus. He follows unwillingly. Again and again he turns his grey head back to the stable, from which the first flames are curling, he stamps his graceful black varnished hooves on the hot cobble stones as if he wants to stay. But finally he submits. The others follow, soon they are all accounted for. They whinny a lot, kick out, prick up their ears, their heads crowd together. But they do not separate from one another. The Master has just returned. The fire brigade of the nearest town has been informed that it must come immediately. Meanwhile our fire-ladders are being brought up. We all pray to heaven that it will not be necessary to employ them. For they are very short and would hardly reach beyond the first storey. Nothing has changed. The sun is low in the sky. But now, strangely enough still in the middle of the conflagration, everyone heaves a sigh of relief, as if the worst is over, everything saved, the damage not too great. People have drawn back from the vicinity of the flames which beat as if with giant wings.

I am on the point of relieving the Duke of command at the pump, when he counts the boys who are formally entrusted to him. For a long time the figure does not tally, because a couple of boys, suffering from headaches from the fumes of the fire, have taken refuge in the meadows behind the houses and belatedly stand up sullenly to report. It is very strange that not one of them wants to make the slightest move towards the main building, for example to save something of their effects or mementos. And up to this time the big house was unaffected by fire, the stairs and corridors could still be traversed without risk. They do not give it a thought, however, and, especially the younger ones, let their pale heads hang like broken flowers.

On the lawn beside the tennis court the "indestructible official", the Bookkeeper, rolls on the ground sobbing compulsively and tearing his worn-out clothes. I stop his mouth, which is overflowing with prayers and self-accusations, and order him, for his childrens' sake, to be silent. But he is deaf, nothing touches him, until I remember the names of his children (or at least some of them) and shout, "Jeanette, Paul, Chéri!" in his ear; now at last he is silent and, as if distracted, runs his finger over the holes which he himself has torn in the threadbare garments. It is overcast and dark, although not yet dusk. A thunderstorm seems to be on the way, the sky against which uncurbed flames beat, spreads out above the school as if lined with a sickly yellow fell.

It makes me proud that the people and the animals have been successfully saved. I would once more like to boldly repeat my entry into the burning building, regardless of all danger, despite the ever brooding fear of D. The dream, the fire in the dream was darker. It ended badly, I know it. At this moment the Duke calls me. In his face I observe with dismay a deep pallor showing through his greenish-yellow bilious complexion. He orders me to him with the curious motion of his hand. "Where is the boy?" he asks quietly. I answer, it is true, "Which boy?" but know immediately exactly whom he means. And now at last terrible dream and reality have become one. I locked little Alma into the fencing room. I forgot it. Who in me forgot it? The one hungry for life? The one fearful of death? I collapse. The heavy key in my trouser pocket crushes my body, but this pain is nothing against my feeling at this moment as, in falling, my knees touch the sharp stones of the courtyard.

Prince Piggy, my old enemy, pulls me to my feet. Titurel stands beside him with his cold, malicious smile. The Duke presses his lips tightly together till all colour has faded from them. He takes me by the hand, forces me by his gaze, to pull out the key, and says to me under his breath, just as this morning, before noon, he said to poor Alma, "Jump to it! On you go!" He drags me through already quite abandoned, stupefyingly hot places, which, in the glare of the leaping flames, I no longer properly recognise. Is this where I have lived for so many years and from today shall no longer live?

Already we are standing at the entrance of the main building. I look up at the window, behind which Alma sits imprisoned. Why does he not fling open the window casements? Why has he not long ago called for help? A malicious, a cunning voice inside me tries to interpret this as if he had nevertheless made his escape through locked doors "by Christ's blood and the mercy of God", which otherwise I have always doubted. But the other voice, the one with the courage to face life, tells me, that I will not be spared this test, that our poor Alma has fallen asleep, numbed by the heat, that he must be lying unconscious on his bench, and that if *we* do not come, his seconds are numbered. For thick smoke already curls around our feet. What shall now be decisive for me? I know what must be done, but I cannot do it! From far away comes the bell of the nearby town's fire brigade. The bell on their vehicle resembles in sound the hand bell of the milkman which woke me and freed me from the terrors of the night, when I was a child sleeping on the crescent shaped sofa. It is only a dream after all, I say to myself. Never fear! One dream more to put beside the others, and from now on, after this last step, all dreams renounced! Off you go! Get a move on! Take a hold of yourself Don't you have a spark of courage? The cloud around us grows ever thicker, it already reaches to our shoulders, and its odour grows ever more poisonous. "It must be done," I say out loud. "Off you go!" Cowardice is more dangerous than courage, but now the other, more prudent, more contemptible self whispers: Are there no others here? You must save yourself for the sake of your family! Your father will die, if you perish. Should two people die? Is a rescue even logically possible at all? Either Alma has already suffocated, or he has already made his escape. He will not calmly have awaited the end sitting in the darkened room. Then again: It must be done!! For who else is there, who dares do it? But I am trembling, I am like wet hemp. Against my will, or only with the will of the one self, my lips form the words "I'm sorry!" I totter helplessly, while my whole body is bathed in icy sweat, shivering in the roaring glow of the flames. Today the wind is stronger than ever. I shiver, for I am afraid. Fear cannot be described, fear like this can only be experienced.

Now we all stand in the courtyard, hot specks of ash drifting down on us, hands protectively over our eyes. Complete silence in the middle of the roaring fire. Even the bells of the fire brigade have fallen silent . . .

I turn to the Duke. I hold the key in my hand. The first faint gold of the fire shimmers on its smooth, iron grey surface. The Duke too is silent, and his silence is proof that he also does not have courage enough. But I? The involuntary trembling of my body, the sinking of my head, from which my cap has fallen, does this not say everything? The Prince has made up his mind more quickly than the two of us, the Duke and I. He snatches the key from my hand. He spits repeatedly into his handkerchief, he holds it like a mask in front of his white, plump face. He narrows his jam coloured little eyes and flies so quickly up the stairs, that it looks as if the wind is blowing him over the steps like a piece of grey paper.

Big, grey, sweat-covered nags with foaming mouths snort and stamp angrily beside me, the fire brigade from V., the factory volunteer force. The first jet of their far from gigantic fire engine is directed at the window on the third floor, which is just being smashed open by a rapier and at which the Prince's head and something white, evidently the upper part of Alma's body in a white shirt, show themselves.

7

But only a second later they have disappeared. Everyone stares up breathless. The steam fire engine, only gradually reaching its full effectiveness, begins to work rhythmically and to emit tall clouds of steam which are caught in the fierily glinting crowns of our beautiful trees. But enough of trees. The fire alone dominates everything. There is a dull rumbling inside the school, as if heavy furniture or chests were being rolled down the steps, and all of a sudden there is a threatening clap of thunder from inside and a flaming mass of material can be seen pouring down the stone stairway which we mounted year after year, day after day. How shall our unfortunate comrades get back? Was everything in vain? For nothing the valour of brave Piggy, the true man, the real hero?

Now Alma's little head is visible for the second time, the Prince's arm around it – a precautionary, reassuring gesture, no different from when, seven years ago, my dear father put his arm around my boyish neck as the two of us watched the Corpus Christi procession from the window of the drawing-room of our apartment in Brussels, at the front the archbishop, the court . . .

In vain do I try at this terrible moment to cling to the

past, do not want to believe what I indeed see before me, do not want to join in the shrill shouting and screaming of the people all around, who are waving at the two unfortunate boys up there and are telling them to remain calm, not to lose heart – all of them no less cowardly and contemptible than I. But they are not Orlamündes, an Orlamünde am I alone. I too, the most cowardly, wave to them with my gloves, the old white ones, which are black and charred in places on the back of the hand. I pull them off, the marks of my elevated rank, which by my cowardice I have forfeited to myself, but the movement hurts me, and when I have at last drawn them off, I see that round pieces of skin have been pulled off at the same time. There are burns, which I got in saving the Bookkeeper, all over my hands. But this physical pain, even if it grows more irritating, more torment-ing with every moment, is as nothing against the feeling of shame. No one accuses me. No one approaches me. Around me is a wide, empty circle, into which are blown only golden sparks, flakes of glowing ash, which the wind does not allow to settle. I shield my eyes from them – or hide my eyes from the unforgettable, indescribable scene, as Alma and the Prince by turns disappear inside the burning room, then come to the windows again, wave and call something inaud-ible. A handkerchief slips from their hands, or is it a piece of paper, a message? It bursts into flame on the way and does not reach us.

The firemen are not standing idly by. The fire master, a fat, slow-moving man with a copper-brown face, has first of all cordoned off the area of the fire. Everyone, the Head-master, the Duke, the pupils, the servants, the school doctor, who saved only his black box with the first-aid kit, the Abbé, the tutors, everyone has been ordered back, I alone have been forgotten. Or are they avoiding me? They direct the hose at the threatened window. In vain. The pressure is too weak, the water tank too small, the old-fashioned machine lacks sufficient power. One fireman pulls over the Onderkuhle fire ladder, but it does not reach far enough, it is only a hindrance, it can itself burn.

There is not a moment to be lost now. From the roof there is sometimes a bubbling up, no different from when one puts soda powder in water, only these are not bubbles of water, not a lemony tasting vapour, but spraying particles the colour of red Bordeaux wine, clouds of fiery dust, because the objects in the attics have caught fire. The stair well in flames. The loft likewise beginning to burn. How long can it still be before it spreads from there to the fencing room and the two boys are destroyed, if they have not preferred to open their veins using one of the sharp rapiers and so to avoid the indescribable pain? Why does one of the tried and tested firemen not attempt to storm the building? It is, admittedly, incomprehensible to me, how it could happen, but in the deepest depth of my heart I nevertheless plead with the unknown deity (Christ and his miracles!) for these two lives to be saved and mine too. For I know very well: a return to my comrades is now already impossible, impossible too, that a cowardly, a detestable Orlamünde should face his father again. But every form of life, every one, would be cut short for me, if one of my comrades, Alma or Piggy, should, through my failure, meet his end under the blazing ruins of the House of Onderkuhle. May the house perish! May the trees, the beautiful trees, burn up, may the riding schools, both of them, with their old straw lining on the oval walls burst into flame like tinder, may the chickens roast themselves, may the stables collapse, the whole magnificent estate disappear without trace, only not a single human life must be lost: this my prayer, the first for years, a true one. Not said on my knees, but standing upright. My hands, covered in blisters, I press against one another with all my strength. Does *that* find a hearing? No one at my side, no father, no fatherly friend, no authority, no mother: I am alone with my guilt.

Then the unexpected happens, a rescue at the last moment. I see that a large piece of cloth, held by all the firemen, is being stretched out under the window around which everything is ablaze. Does it not resemble the lining of a cradle, so deep, so soft? Letting go of the jumping sheet, two firemen shout, cupping their hands to their lips. One of them vigorously acts out a suggested movement. Those firemen who are positioned closer to the wall are particularly endangered, for at every moment blazing ruins plunge down, and one understands now why the men wear iron dragoons' helmets, against whose brass crests smaller fragments can glance off without causing any harm.

I hardly recognise the faces of my friends in the window frame through the billowing veil of burning air. But now the wind blows away the strands of flame. One can see everything with the greatest clarity as if through opera glasses.

Little Alma is first. Piggy helps him out of the window, shields him from the glass splinters which still remain, makes him lean out as far as possible, then grips him around the hips, lifts him like a feather out of the window, as far away as possible from the wall, against which the little boy could dash his head, and gives him a brief order, a command, and Alma, who did not have the courage to entrust himself to me at the pole during the swimming lesson, who cried out, "I'm drowning!", risks the terrible dangerous leap, traverses the hot expanse of space, without fear, he knows how to hold himself as he falls. Already he's below, bounces up once again, half hidden in the undulating folds of the sheet. The firemens' heads are brought a little closer together by the tug of the cloth; I experience this rescue with indescribable emotion, and at the same time I am aware that I have lived through this once before (that is, as dream).

Now, as Alma forces his way out of the tumult quick as a little weasel and laughing(!), and as the light of the leaping flames strokes his little fine haired head, now the much larger Prince swings himself out of the window; he pushes away with his elbows and fists to prevent himself from colliding with the wall. Already he has reached the bottom, much more clumsily than the boy, and the heads of the men holding the blanket crack into one another. I cannot laugh, but I draw a deep breath of relief. It was this, that I saw in the dreams of recent nights. The Prince pushes his way through the crowd of firemen. He does not see me. He joins the others, walking slowly, stifling a smile on his dark lips, crossing the courtyard with tired, unequal steps.

Now the work of the fire brigade has been completed. The excitedly wheezing pump is helpless. The house is lost. The firemen must withdraw, try to protect those of the surrounding buildings which are not yet burning. The horses snort, their glittering hooves stamp on the school flags which someone has rescued and left lying on the ground, their tails beat nervously back and forward. The men lead them away. They step firmly and safely on the glowing ground in their high boots, they disregard the flags, let them smoulder and perish. From time to time one of them glances back, lifts his crested helmet from a sweat-soaked but nevertheless pale forehead and walks on more quickly. It is the middle of the night. No moon. No stars. Only heat and wind.

Soon the courtyard is empty. The fire is no longer at the angry stage and is now pacified.

Suddenly the whole roof lifts up, as if it were made of paper, remains there for a second and collapses twinkling like a firework. Then the walls begin to glow. The bright flames, the licking and crackling has gone. Calmly and solemnly, the whole huge building, the home of my youth, is silently burning down.

8

I shall never forget the walk through burning Onderkuhle. Behind me on the bright hill, blazing without a sound, as if bathed in liquid bronze, the main building, swarms of birds circling above it, before me the brilliantly illuminated park. The clouds of smoke have become caught in the crowns of the beautiful trees, beneath which, with every moment that passes, more people gather. For many years only dependants of the aristocratic college have trod in these places, now people have poured in from the whole neighbourhood, in their midst my comrades, then the tutors. Policemen too have arrived and with threatening expressions surround the Master. He directs them to me, and I report what I know: that the fire started in the accounts office, that fuel flowed out of the petrol tank of a motorcycle and caught fire. I am prepared to swear to it. It is clear to everyone. The Master, who expresses his thanks with a measured bow, is set free. He knows how to maintain his self-control, unlike the Head-master, who rambles on about the burnt blue school flags. For has not our whole life been burnt and turned to ashes on this day, the 29th of June? Mine at least has been. With my face hidden, in my hands the burnt gloves, marked with black circles, I take the darkest path through the farm, but encounter another fire brigade just arriving, the one from the neighbouring estate. The landlord is a Herculean man, who never loses his sense of humour. He too is a former pupil of our establishment and, rare indeed, non-aristocratic. He recognises me immediately and holds me fast with his powerful farmer's fist, as he gives his labourers instructions regarding the fire pump. But there will not be much that can be done, as the Master remarks, since the steam pump and ours are already connected to the few hydrants that can provide water. The Master and Mr B. know one another, Mr B. has often invited the Master to go hunting, as if he were his equal. Now too they speak quietly to one another like brothers.

Our chapel is lit up from inside, as if a mass were being held here. The riding school is only a wreath of flames. I take advantage of the moment and make my escape, lose myself deeper in that part of the park in which the animals are tethered. The cattle are lethargic, they have settled down, the many creases of their sagging stomachs have taken on a reddish tint from the fire. They eat the dried up grass which has almost turned into hay, grind it and chew the cud, rattling their heavy iron chains. The bull's dull-sounding bell tolls. The warmed skin hangs in folds from the evenly breathing breasts, flickering brightly. Despite the fire they all appear calm. The continuing humming of the fire is clearly heard, interrupted from time to time by a muffled thunder, which marks the collapse of a stairway, a traverse, a wall. Unlike the large-eyed cattle I do not look calmly towards the fire. Like the horses I have timidly turned away, my eyes are watering. No, I am not weeping, for at regular intervals, without true spiritual convulsion, one salty drop after another collects in the corners of my eyes and runs down from there. My friend Titurel passes me by, arm in arm with the Prince. The Prince limps a little, both do and do not see me. The horses are nervous, they rub against one another, open their mouths, as if they wanted to yawn, they whinny, they search for something with their long, raised, swan-like necks, they gaze helplessly and distractedly, they twist round, want to get away, and with their snag teeth nibble at the trees which hold them fast, destroy the bark, scrape the earth at their feet. From here in the fields the distant flames flicker golden and mellow. Not one touches the hay which the compassionate stable boy has spread out at their feet. They are not well disposed to one another, although they press closely together, they kick and bite, their ears are pinned back, and one of them, my beloved Cyrus, has, in his sense-less fear, thrown himself to the ground, and is in danger of throttling himself, since the leather bridle binds him and has already made a deep furrow in his silky soft, fine grey skin. At the same time he kicks out with all four legs in uncontrol-lable fury. His huge body has squashed everything flat, the more delicate bushes, whose first fruits shine in the glow of the distant fire like golden grapes, flattened as if in the herbarium press. As the light falls on different parts of his belly, covered with swollen veins, I recognise the danger the animal faces; I guard myself as well as I can against the struggling rear legs, with their sharp edged horseshoes, I am quickly at the horse's head, unbridle the horse by undoing the strap, coax him, for I know that even at moments of great excitement horses are responsive to the human voice. The animal immediately becomes calmer, gets up, first on its front legs and then, bouncing up like a ball, on its splendid hind legs and stands beside me, snorting loudly, gleaming gold and grey, as if cast in metal. He rubs his still trembling nostrils against my pike grey jacket and whinnies softly at me.

Something fire-coloured twists at my feet. Now the fire cat utters its long drawn-out wails, whimpering like a little child. It has been expelled for ever from its house, to which such animals become more attached than to the most beloved people. Why did it not surrender completely to the fire? It follows us, myself and Cyrus, whom I lead further into the darkness, but soon it turns away from me with yet more melancholy, gentle cries and bounds back to the burning house, but soon runs after me again, tail erect, the big mouth wide open as it cries, so that one can see all the pointed teeth and the big ridged tongue. So neither of the animals wants to leave me.

I, however, want to be alone, I must be alone, a weight lies on my breast, perhaps only the weight of the heavy, stinging smoke I have inhaled, since I feel lighter with every exhalation and with every inhalation a weight once more lies in the pit of my stomach. I did not know then what sorrow is like. Only this was it. Were a stranger to see me, perhaps Titurel or Prince Piggy, then he would think I were completely broken, fallen to pieces entirely. But it was not so. An Orlamünde cannot quite forget himself. Now it appears so only as a consequence of my casual bearing, I behave as if I were coming from a lengthy walk or from an arduous riding lesson – so I drag myself along the gravel strewn path which leads out of the park.

I mount, my horse Cyrus calmly stands still; although I no longer have any brute power over the animal, he submits easily to me. I remain a man even at this hour, a horseman even in this place, in this burning, dying home. It is dark under the lime trees of the avenue, for the light of the fire only penetrates faintly through the dense roof on to the neck and the short mane of the horse in front of me and also on to my ungloved hands, which are beginning to hurt badly.

The pain is most easy to bear if I raise my hands to shoulder height and maintain myself on the tall horse solely by pressure of the thighs. Cyrus begins to trot gently of his own accord. Far behind us the scene of the blaze, from which are faintly heard the horn signals of the estate fire brigade. So we continue along the ever more strongly scented avenue of lime trees, almost black beneath the storm clouds, past the for ever abandoned playing fields of the burning school. Now I must cross a small wooden bridge which booms under the animal's hooves like the drum of a wild Congo tribe. At the bend in the path, a dark red light falls on us. The horse starts at the glare, he increases his speed for a short gallop. Many leaves are falling. Drought, summer heat and early autumn in one. A hot, strong wind begins to whirl them round and lift them into the air.

As fast as the horse is going, I nevertheless attempt to throw a glance behind me. I catch sight of our school building, without a roof, with the walls half broken down, from which bright flames shoot up; the further one goes, the taller it seems to stand out against the utterly dark night sky. Did all this not happen once before? It will never be again. I shall no longer live there. The regular, rocking, rising and falling, up and down of the gallop will calm me. But if Cyrus's hoof strikes a stone, it goes straight to my heart, not without pain.

Now the school with its envelope of flame has completely disappeared, we ride on under young beeches which only softly breathe and whisper in the sultry summer breeze. Here comes the avenue of poplars, and there's a turn uphill. Under the sober green of the conifers appears the first reflection of the nocturnal lake. A dim, red cloudy sky pierced by sparkling stars drives the crowns of the trees, shivering in the eternal breath of wind, together, the track opens out, the outflow of the distant gold tinged lake thunders over the weir with a muffled drum beat. The trumpets blare, they sound like reveilles or the final signals at the close of an exercise. Is it the end of all attempts to extinguish the fire? Through the fragrant breath of the forest wafts something of the heavy, poisonous smell of the fire. We bump against tall, soft haystacks. Quite without strength I am now only clinging to the horse. I slip down. I lie in the strongly scented hay. Over me the big stone grey eyes of the horse. The water is disturbed, the waves beat regularly against the shore. Many birds are astir in the nearby wood, awakened by the fire. A few have risen, have flown over the surface of the water. Their outspread wings show the golden reflection of the fire of Onderkuhle, or is it the late rising, enormous copper coloured moon? I turn my face away from the horse, quietly pulling at the grass, bury my face in my sleeve and cry my first tears, and not the last.

PART THREE

1

So ends Onderkuhle. So ends my aristocratic education.

Where to? Back to my parents? What can I be to them, if not a burden? A son belongs with his parents, I know that. But what if he only adds grief to their princely troubles? They have passed on the gift of poverty and frugality to me, but they have kept enough for themselves. And yet they would not shut the door on their only son, even if he did not return to them in the full glory of an excellent report. They would chop their small portions in even smaller pieces, perhaps allot me the largest share, but bear all the troubles themselves, as now too they prefer to keep their troubles to themselves, instead of writing to me. For their silence is not absence of love. But let them be blinded by their love, I am not by my love.

I follow the path between the beet fields that leads to the nearest larger town. I have taken my leave of Onderkuhle. I see only too clearly that this leavetaking falls short of the laws acknowledged by myself. Not to be courageous, but to show courage was what was demanded. It is not always possible to be courageous, it is always possible to show courage. That was the rule of the school and of the Master. What I was, I have destroyed. Should it have been so? Should

I thank fate, that it has destroyed Onderkuhle, and together with beautiful Onderkuhle, tended and loved for generations, also the Onderkuhle in myself? I live. I feel, cowardice is more dangerous than courage. I want to risk the attempt to live alone, to get by alone. My hands no longer hurt. Skin has already begun to grow over the open wounds. I am eighteen years old. My identity papers are in my breast pocket and my watch is in my left side pocket. In V. it will be possible to convert it into money, that is the most important thing to begin with. It will not be much, but enough to get me to Brussels and to keep my head above water there for the first few days.

The flat countryside I am traversing has long ago lost its peculiar Onderkuhle character. There are fields, hamlets, farms, tracks and herds of cattle as everywhere in the world. But with a feeling of the most joyful amazement I suddenly see before me, at seven o'clock in the morning, the fata morgana as I saw it a few days before the accident: part of a town, V. in fact, at its edge a fairly high but discoloured factory wall, clearly crumbling in places. The building stands alone, is surrounded by unpleasant fumes, reminiscent of the smell of chlorine during the chemistry experiments in Onderkuhle. I see a wide gate, which is just opening, in order to admit the exhausted firemen on their motor truck, later followed by a horse drawn fire engine. The motor vehicle rolls along slowly, the horses, however, are panting, they have given their utmost to follow the truck. Further to the rear of the factory, smoke is coming from a rectangular, relatively tall chimney, it too showing signs of decay. Perhaps the chemical fumes are corrosive. Also far and wide around the building everything green is stunted and sparse. It is a weekday and work is beginning as always. The workers look at me, they know where I come from. Every shopkeeper in the little town, where all the suppliers of the college live, knows it too. When I enter the very first shop and put down my watch, in order to obtain money for it, the watch is refused, but every sum requested is placed at my disposal without security and even – very Onderkuhle – a written note as I.O.U. is refused. But I insist. Then I make my way to the railway station. A train, from which even more workers for the factory alight, is just pulling in. My pike grey uniform is recognised, and a young factory girl smiles at me, half friendly, half mocking. I buy my ticket on the train and in the late afternoon of the same day am in my native city.

It is hot, but the air is heavy with damp. The bright sunshine bursts through into the excessively crowded streets as if into shafts. But here on the broad boulevards it is no easier to breathe than in the vicinity of the poisonous clouds of chlorine produced by the factory in V. The traffic, to me almost incomprehensibly loud and fast, passes in the midst of a kind of glittering fog from which only the dusty grey crowns of the pitiable trees and the towers of the old edifices protrude. The streets and squares are filled to overflowing with harassed people, who are nevertheless not even properly exhausted, in addition vehicle upon vehicle with wretched, blindly rushing horses, automobiles driven along at furious speed. I hardly recognise again the streets which I neverthe-less saw countless times as a child. In a very narrow sidestreet, which, however, consists entirely of six storey buildings, I find a lodging house, where one can have a bedroom for very little money. Here also there is a set of house-rules, stuck up on the brightest wall of the dark little chamber, which contains the invitation to participate daily in the bless-ings of prayer together. But no compulsion is exercised. The house itself is as calm amid the frantic roar of the streets as a large pebble in the middle of a beehive. Just this stillness is hard to bear. I am tired, but incapable of sleeping a wink. I had thought it would be easier to live in the same city as my parents, without already seeking them out in the first hour. I would too much like to risk drawing closer to my parents even today. The mere possibility makes me happy, happier than I was lately in Onderkuhle.

2

Is it not as if my father had taken me to the station only yesterday? Today I return. I imagine he has received the news of my arrival too late, or he has been prevented from coming to the station, an important session at the club of the nobility detains him. Thus do I try to distract myself from the worries, which – only now do I feel it so clearly – have weighed on me in recent weeks. My mother I do not count on even in my imagination. *Her* I do not expect even in my dreams. Already I have hurried through the streets between the station and my home. Suddenly I am struck by the thought: has my father met with an accident? Does a punishment await me for my failure? In our college there were never any serious punishments. Very often the pupils themselves carried out a punishment, but a chastisement was never ordered by one of the teachers or masters; the most severe punishment was confinement in a locked room, alone with oneself and one's bad conscience.

All these thoughts are extinguished in an instant, when I catch sight of a hearse at the door of my home. It is not mortal fear that overcomes me, it is rather a hot fear, a live terror. I do not feel compelled to lament, utter cries, moan, nor to prostrate myself on the steps, but I feel forced to avert my gaze and, I confess it, to take flight. What has happened? Before what does the man want to flee, who has only just fled before the fire of Onderkuhle? For whom is the hearse, with the tired, sweaty, wiry horses, which are covered in shabby, once black, now green tinged caparisons, waiting in the late afternoon light? Who is it? My playful, gentle, shy, girlish mother, who had only one fault, to shrink back from touching me? But do I not likewise shrink from her? Is my reserve not so great that I draw back into the entrance of the house opposite? There I breathe in with relief the cool air, filled with the faint smell of fruit. Or is it my eternally weary father, the Prince with the drooping lip, the slate coloured eyes, which all too rarely change to blue? An aloof man, conscious of his noble rank, with a gentlemanly gait. His hands, which are always ready to give, are unfortunately often empty, rarely, however, does he remove his gloves.

On the stairway the few wall lamps are burning, there is a peculiar twilight, since a bright ray of the evening sun (how clearly I now see the house before me!) falls from the courtyard windows. It looks as if someone had forgotten to turn off the light. A dark green mourning carpet has been stretched over the runner as well. It shows up traces of dirt and dust, deliverymen and residents cannot be prevented from ascending, even if on tiptoe in view of the solemn occasion.

It cannot be that a member of our family is waiting to be buried. Or have the troubles of our house reached the point that it can no longer afford a death appropriate to noble rank? I now feel the closeness of my parents as something very close, very familiar, very warm, reassuring, not as something upsetting. And yet I would like to shed tears for both of them.

When I longed for them in Onderkuhle, I never became so aware of my sympathy as now, when, from the entrance of the house opposite, I look at the doubly illuminated stairs bathed in bright dust. But should I weep for people, who for so many years I have either not seen at all, like my mother, or only for a few strictly supervised moments, like my father? But indescribable, nothing less than indescribable, is my joy as I now catch sight of them both! My mother descends a few steps in front, as if she cannot wait to reach the street, she is followed by my father, very serious, very pale. Behind them the bearers, bearded, already elderly figures, who, not without effort, carefully carry a black coffin. It must be our ancient servant David whom they are now going to inter. Probably he was ill for a long time, my poor father served him, rather than that he had served my father, but they did not wish to part. Hence the long silence. Only because of that? If I could only believe it! My father is very moved, he tries to compose himself, looks round, to make sure the coffin is being handled properly – a pointless movement, but very affecting, since my father is wearing a white collar which is far too high and can only move his head with difficulty. Now both my parents sob loudly, they weep as soon as they step out of the house. Not for me, who is watching them from his corner and encloses them both with his timid love. Now they all pass close by me. I see before me the coffin made of cheap material, from which the varnish is cracking, I see, as only decoration, the meagre wreath of flowers with the blue silk bow. My father now turns to my mother, to offer her his arm. I make use of this moment to step out of the entrance and bow low. Only thus can I conceal myself from them. And must I not? Does it not have to be so? In Catholic countries it is the custom to salute every funeral by removing one's hat. Never was a more empty salutation made nor accepted. I, the living son, let my living parents pass without a word, but I greet the dead servant for the sake of his death. Or for the sake of the service he gave? My parents see me but they do not recognise me. Only thus is to be explained the wordless expression of thanks, which they both favour me with, my father more warmly, my mother with rather greater detachment. So we met again after such a long time! It is almost seven years since I saw my mother. She has hardly aged, she is beautiful, as she always was, but my father displays a completely altered appearance.

The sliding shelf on the hearse is pulled out very quickly, laden with the coffin and shoved in again. A strange sight, which is not without a comic aspect, for it looks as if a square loaf were being shoved into the oven. Now a heavy coach, which has been waiting at a shadowy corner under the wispy trees, is driven up. The coachman is just as tired as the undertakers' men. Evidently they already have more than one third class burial behind them today, quickly the men gather up the mourning carpet as well, turn out the lights, bring down in a hurry two iron candelabra, which they store away under the sliding shelf with the rest of the solemn junk, and now they strike the horses, they want to get to the churchyard and then home to their families.

My parents have taken their seats in the old-fashioned, long and curved, but very well sprung carriage, which now, as it picks up more speed, rocks like a boat at sea. So, with inappropriate haste, they follow the body of their old servant. He was also the companion of my early years, caring for me dependably but without love. He was loyal to the House of Orlamünde, not to me. He had been servant to three generations. Is that why he must have a third class burial? I am serious, not ironic, which is quite alien to me. Each generation lived in accordance with the family's station, in so far as it could. The fourth before me still in possession of a great fortune and on its own land. But my grandfather, the only offspring of my great-grandfather (there were no prolific marriages among all of our kinsfolk), already consumed much, acquired nothing, he married into straitened circumstances, my father into distressed ones. All three generations had servants, the oldest a large number, the second a middling number, of which in the end only the old boy remained. I shall no longer lay claim to his services. I shall be my own servant and, if luck will have it, my own master too. But the tradition of our house, I know it, is being borne towards the churchyard under the flaking varnish of his pinewood coffin by that very carriage, whose horses sweat under their cotton caparisons. Here too an Orlamünde goes the way of our declining family. I do not want to follow him.

As I take the old familiar steps of our apartment with a few leaps, I joyfully feel the cloth of my undress jacket pressed against my breast, such an awareness of life has hold of me now. I have to decide what I must do next. Only manual labour can support me. I am strong, young and healthy, without demands, without doubts, for I am afraid of nothing. Machines, proletarian labour for little money, even physical contact with men, none of it alarms me. Above all, I want to make my way by my own efforts. Why should what millions of others manage be impossible just for me?

One more generation, my own, the fourth, would have been able to cling to the remnants of princely magnificence, even if only either commoners in spirit or with wretched results. I know that my mother owns a valuable pearl necklace. My father has a pair of golden spurs, an old cuirass inlaid with steel and gold, ancient orders with genuine, if small, stones, cut in an old-fashioned way and our name. He still owns the name, what is left of the other treasures I do not know and I do not want to know. For I consciously wish to renounce every inheritance. Now I want to regard myself as missing; I fled from Onderkuhle, in the wide world, from which nothing separates me and from which, against my will, nothing can hold me back, I am never more to be found. The other way is less romantic. But it is more human and spares my parents the great distress of searching at length and in vain for me. I only have to disappear like a man in the crowd. But with the best son's will in the world I cannot spare them this pain, of parting from them, even if only for the present, and leaving them to their fate and myself to mine. Presumably they do not yet know anything of my fate. They rarely read newspapers and the School Headmaster of Onderkuhle has probably not yet sent them any news. It is better if they are told everything, which they must be told anyway, by me. I want to write to my family and also trace out my path through life in the near future as on a time table in Onderkuhle. I am leaning with my shoulders against the door of our apartment, through which seeps the old aroma of the parental home and with it the quite delicate exhalation of incense, of slaked lime, of medicine and death. By chance I have some paper with me (what pupil of an educational establishment is without a notebook, even if he had nothing to write?), and now I write: "Dear, most beloved parents! On the twenty-ninth of June our college in Onderkuhle fell victim to a conflagration. We were all, teachers and staff and pupils, saved, likewise the horses. On the following morning I departed by way of V. and arrived here at five seventeen p.m. I immediately had the great joy of seeing you both. This reassures me greatly. The absence of your letters for such a long time troubled me. Now everything is all right. I must now endeavour to take up a profession, and hope that I shall soon succeed in this. I have a favour to ask of you. Please do not look for me! I must first of all put everything in order, then I shall present myself immediately. And something else, a real request, which matters far more to me than the first: I would very much wish, that you . . ." I cross this sentence out. I reflect on what I have, what I lack, what I desire. At the thought of the first freedom in my life, my heart leapt, I cannot put it any other way. In Onderkuhle I lived well, but I was not free. The air here, which on arrival in the city seemed to me poisonously chlorine-like, now seems to me wonderfully light, life-giving and intoxicating. So it is, that I write something that is not in the spirit of my upbringing, is not in accordance with the Master's rule of distance.

But I feel it so: "I know, beloved parents, that you still own valuable jewellery and the like, which you are unable to part with, perhaps solely out of concern for my future. This concern has now been removed. Sell, if need be, these objects, which now as in the future, would only be a burden to me, and if my request means anything to you, do not economise, in order one day to leave me something. My plans are good, and I hope that I shall not only be able to support myself, but can also put something aside for my further education. I hope that I shall see you again soon. Do not worry! I want to make the attempt to live alone. Whether the attempt succeeds or not, in any event you shall soon see me again. Give me time and do not worry! Do not forget my request!

I kiss my dear mother's hand, I greet my beloved father with profound respect!

Your faithful son

Boëtius."

I push the sheets of paper under the door, where my parents

must find them immediately on returning home. Then I go back along the broad streets to my lodging house. Most shops are already shut, but a few shops close to the station are still open. I first of all buy buttons, which I want to sew on to my jacket in the place of the silver ones, then articles of clothing, a cheap hat and a practical coat. In the railway waiting room I eat a snack, which nevertheless ends up being more expensive than if I had bought bread and cheese or bacon. I enter every expenditure in the notebook.

Meanwhile it has become dusk. I have arrived at the lodging house. Situated in the very quiet alley, in which the thunder of the street noise of the boulevards is only very indistinctly heard, it is now full of life. My little room is clean and tidy, but not very cosy. A pale, illuminated fire wall faces the wide open window. A piece of violet sky can be seen, still somewhat hazy. But as I lie in bed and wait for sleep, this haze dissolves in the approaching coolness of night, and the stars come out, surrounded by light, hovering clouds of indeterminate colour and distinct outline. Today I bear this sight without a feeling of oppression, without panic dismay, without fear. From the milkily illuminated night clouds, presaging the closeness of the still invisible moon, my thoughts pass to Cyrus, who disappeared last night at the lake of Onderkuhle. While I was just falling asleep did he free himself and look for the other horses again? Or, delighting in an unaccustomed freedom, is he now grazing in the broad magnificent meadows along the railway line between Onderkuhle and V.? In one of the rooms giving on to the courtyard of the Christian lodging house, men and women begin a long drawn out monotonous hymn, which is interrupted by words of a sermon. I try in vain to follow the words. I fall asleep over them, dreamless, deep, satisfied.

3

The next morning, waking early, I washed quickly. In the clean, but nevertheless musty smelling breakfast room I get an acceptable breakfast for a few coins. It is still early morning. I do not wait for morning prayers, which are set for six o'clock, but leave the house, with the firm intention of finding work and income. The streets are comparatively free of vehicles, but the pavements are filled by a dense crowd of workers, silently hurrying along, all of whom, whether old or young, display the same shuffling, rather than walking gait and the same look of tiredness. At random I follow a relatively striking figure, a tall pock-marked labourer or artisan or railway employee, whom, despite every effort, however, I lose sight of at the next corner in the crowd. But I continue in the same direction, which seems to lead to the factory quarter of the city. I walk down long streets across which, in the morning sun, falls the long shadow of the tenement blocks. It is still cool, carts with magnificent fruit and a profusion of flowers pass by and spread a beautiful fragrance. I am entering a quarter quite unknown to me from my childhood, which was possibly not even built then. Now one huge factory after another stands here. One shift of workers is just leaving the building by a gate, the other group enters the vast complex which stretches as far as the canal without recognising or greeting anyone from the opposing party. Every one must pass the gatekeeper, a fat, grey-haired man with a short pipe, which has gone out, who, as each man enters, puts a mark on a board, which gleams in the twilight of his cell beside huge cabinets for keys and the face of a time clock. Although this board contains many hundreds of names, not one of those entering needs to wait, but just as little is a stranger admitted. The offices in the administration building have their own entrance, which first leads into a well cared for little garden, then into the fine, but plain brick building. The gatekeeper motions to me as well as to several other younger men. We remain standing to the side so as not to be anyone's way. Everything happens smoothly and as a matter of course. Nothing spoils my elated, almost joyful, mood. At the stroke of six a powerful siren begins to howl and the almost unbearable noise shakes the whole building. Apart from a few stragglers, the whole crowd has disappeared inside the individual factory buildings. Now everything becomes quieter, the rhythmic thundering can be heard more clearly, the deep hum, which sounds as if it comes from underground, short whistles, the rattle of unwinding chains, in the distance the whinnying of a nag or the bell of a tram car, which is probably taking a sharp bend round the block of buildings, making the wheels squeal.

It has happened without any deliberation, that like the other young men I am queueing for work here in this unfamiliar factory. From an office worker we receive a metal tag with letters punched out of it and are directed to a small shed, where a foreman in grey drill overalls is sitting, who takes down our particulars. Then our sight and our hearing is tested, at which I come off best, a couple of questions to test our intelligence are put, which admittedly are strange to me, but which, nevertheless, I manage to solve. Then the notes made are handed to another employee, presumably an engineer, who looks carefully at everything with his deep set eyes, but discovers nothing out of the ordinary, neither with regard to me nor to the others. In a flat voice, as if he was drawing lots for a party game, he asks, "Skilled? Unskilled? Office? Fitter? Draughtsman? Apprenticeship? Electrician? Winder? Labourer? Toolmaker? Milling machine operator? Driver? Pattern maker?" He seems to need precisely these accomplishments, unfortunately none of us is suitable for them. I do not know for what I should volunteer. Finally he returns to his lists again and hands some of us new metal tokens. The latter proceed, after they have glanced at the tokens, to a part of the huge complex which consists of innumerable improvised sheds, roofed with corrugated iron, then again of halls like church naves, constructed as if for ever. In between them there are garages and store rooms of reinforced concrete, small gauge railway tracks with completely marshalled trains, many waggons, one after the other loaded with pieces of machinery, evidently dynamos and turbines, if my limited technical knowledge does not deceive me. Now work is in full swing everywhere. There is a great bustle in the factory yards. Trucks roll out of the buildings. Squealing and whistling, emitting large clouds of steam and behaving like big express train engines, the small locomotives move off, heading for the sidings of the state railway. The noise grows ever shriller. Amid it the monotonous roaring and thumping of the machines can be felt rather than heard. The air is full of fine dust and smoke, of the strange aroma that was noticeable near the school, when on very hot days the railway sleepers and tracks at Onderkuhle burned under the hot sun. Helplessly I stray back and forward between factory buildings and sheds. To me this is a completely strange world, whose necessity and purposefulness, however, is quickly evident to me. Suddenly I am standing at a canal basin where huge flat barges or lighters with timber wait ready to unload. They rock sluggishly on the waves. The fragrant woodland scent of the resinous trunks mingles with the somewhat musty smell of the stagnant water, on whose surface there is an iridescent film of brightly coloured oil. Unharnessed and motionless, with drooping heads, a pair of old but good horses stand beside the timber and do not look up. They doze idly in the morning sun, only now and then striking out at swarming flies with their oddly short-trimmed, helpless tails.

I am right at the edge of the factory area and certainly not where there is labouring work (Assembly, Token P) for me. So I return to my starting point again, remembering that the newest as well as the tallest building, the church nave-like, bright red edifice with the large windows and the steep, dull blue slate roof was by the entrance. Chance has it that that is just where I am expected. For I enter through the revolving door unchecked. The hall is at least as high as a three storey house. It does not have proper walls, only iron frames which are brick faced on the outside, undisguised inside, and between them glass walls of large ribbed panes, these are not the tiny school exercise book sized window-panes that are usual in factory buildings. A single room under a sharp angled roof: dozens of machine parts, rotating, swinging back and forth, pounding and sliding, of almost naked, pale mens' bodies, of cranes dipping, swinging and turning, whose silvery, shining chains move through the hall like arms, everything enveloped in a cloud of fine dust, like a sandy racetrack, through which fly stray sparks and the blueish bundles of flame which issue from a blowtorch. At least two hundred workers are employed in the hall. One does not understand how they set about things, sees only that everything moves and progresses. Against the short wall of the hall stand cube shaped steel structures, about the size of a peasant hut, their colour shimmering between grey and blue. From their centre appear, simultaneously coming closer and becoming thinner, fish shaped pieces of iron, the width of a hundred year old oak, from which a kind of plane shaves off spiral strips with a shriek, in a similar way to the mechanical potato peeler in the hand of a kitchen servant in Onderkuhle, although here the potato peels itself, as it were. Other machine tools bore holes at marked points in iron plates as thick as a fist, as if it were soft cheese. Workers in sand coloured overalls crouch on the oil smeared asphalt floor which is, however, often sprinkled with water. In chalk they copy on to the unprepared workpieces, on a large scale, with their compasses and folding rules, what is decreed on the blue marked plans of the engineers. While one was not taking any notice, the fish-like piece has freed itself from the machine, which all at once stands still. The buzzing jaws of an electric crane coming down from above approach it, grip it, under the supervision of a charge hand, carry it away over the unconcerned, sweat-covered heads of the workers to another part of the hall, which is now filled with bright sunshine. Here, with a noise inaudible in the din, it is loaded on to one of the small gauge railway wagons, on which there are beams ready, to which the piece is chained or riveted. It is only temporarily fastened to the beam and now goes to another machine shop.

The workers' faces are imperturbable. They have an expression which I have never seen on peasants or the servants of our college. The men arrive in the morning evidently already weary of labour. They do not speak, they do not smoke, they tell no jokes, they do not amuse themselves, although they are not constantly employed, are not at all "tied down". They stand there apparently indifferent, until it is their turn and they must carry out a particular manual operation. But this they accomplish in such a way with every ounce of their strength, that the muscles of the naked upper arms brace audibly and sweat drips from eyelids into the corners of the mouths and from the back of the head on to the neck. One man lies on the floor and looks at a piece from below, like an astronomer into a telescope, and in a voice which is inaudible, but nevertheless comprehensible to those standing around him, gives instructions which the people immediately mark with chalk on the workpiece.

4

I have been observed long ago, but no one has moved from his place. There seems also not to be any senior supervisory person in the hall, at least I am unable to distinguish them from the others. I wander through the huge room, until I have reached the foot of a framework, the base of one of the many cranes, which with their long necks, their glittering chains and their tiny drivers' cabins, only accessible by iron ladders, rise above the floor of the assembly shop. Here I am called. Not with a proper shout, but with a whistle, as if I were a little dog. But who knows my name here? It is meant for me. I have understood the signal and as a good gymnast climb nimbly up the somewhat slippery ladder, I make a bow to the crane driver, who does not, however, take any further notice of me. Without taking his eyes off the drop below him, he holds out his left hand to me. The right is holding the steering wheel. But he expects no comradely handshake from me, and has only stretched out his hand to receive the token which was handed over to me earlier. He does not speak to me. Perhaps he does not know that I am to be employed here for the first time, but perhaps every communication would be impossible in all the din. (Later I saw that one could also converse here, at any rate it was not necessary to raise one's voice much at all. How it was possible, I do not know.) Now he points to the right, to the corner of the little cabin which smells of oil and is bespattered with wet tobacco remains, in which there is a tin oil can and a couple of rough cloths. He operates the crane uninterruptedly. Turns it outwards, inwards, raises it, lowers it, all of it accurate to a centimetre, to a half second. He works almost silently with his heavy chains, he is a master of his trade. As soon as there is a breathing space he instructs me in my work: open the spring tops on the machine, hold the neck of the oil can against them, squeeze the can firmly at the sides, open other lubrication points by unscrewing the cap, lubricating with solid grease, which is in an old nickel box, scrape away the surplus with a match stick, climb up and down the ladder, position the workpieces better, wrap them in wood-wool, so that they are not damaged in transit. The work which I had to carry out at this time, was only inessential work, like that, for example, which in Onderkuhle was done by the stable-boy. For neither was the actual grooming of horses his duty, for grooming was part of the groom's duties, strictly laid down by the Master and supervised by the riding teachers and by the estate officials, nor was personal attendance on the Master, for the latter was not entitled to it. So the stable-boy was superfluous. I in the turbine factory likewise.

The work of the crane driver, my superior, is not uninterrupted. Often twenty minutes pass while the crane stands idle, only shaken by the noise and vibration of the automatic steam hammers in the neighbouring shop bursting explosively into action, then suddenly falling silent again. During this time the driver could refresh himself with coffee. Alcohol was officially forbidden, that was even pinned up in the reception office and was grounds for immediate dismissal.

When it was the turn of "his" crane, he was given a signal, which he usually did not even need, for he had already started his part hydraulically, part electro magnetically driven machine. The arms reach out, while the crane moves even closer below, the jaws either grip the piece directly, as with smaller pieces, or a large chain, held by a question mark-like connecting piece, is looped round it. There are also, however, grab cranes, which can gather up loose iron parts, to put them into the small wagons. When the mass has been wound up into the air and has reached the highest point, it begins to sway from side to side. The particular skill of the crane driver consists of avoiding these sideways movements as much as possible, since it strains the material of the crane, chain and transmission, and the possibility arises that the load could some time work itself free, although the jaws remain pressed together by electro magnets as long as the current is flowing through. But my chief knows his job, a piece may weigh five tons or a hundred (ship's keels or big turbine shafts), it makes no difference to him. He gets each piece to the required place, without constantly looking at it, simply out of an inborn feeling for the job. Friendliness, however, is not his strong point. He pushes me away with his elbow if I bother him; yet I have already, of my own accord, made myself as little as possible, for the cabin is small.

It is impossible for me to think about Onderkuhle, about my parents, about myself, indeed about anything particular at all during the work (and yet it is not even serious and responsible). Under no circumstances is it possible to compare this work with the work in our school, with the breaking in of a horse, not even of Cyrus. How one can bear such an activity, beginning in adolescent youth until the months before one's death, I do not understand. There must be added want, something that I know exists, but not how. My work is by far the easiest. I have to keep the lubrication points in order; a little oil and cup grease flows out at every operation, it has to be replaced, if necessary the crane driver could take care of it too, and presumably usually does so. The dust has to be wiped from the electrical measuring instrument, the ampere meter, then one has to climb down from time to time, to steady a workpiece, if it is going to swing. Then again, pick one's way through the jumble of machines, small gauge railway tracks and people, who, however, step aside good-naturedly, must run to the works canteen, getting lost in the confusion, fetch coffee in a blue enamel can for the crane driver, also allow oneself something, so as not to collapse, but at the same time watch the clock, so as not to stay away too long. Then again fetch a roll of chewing tobacco, but which is not the desired sort, so "jump" back down again. So midday comes, the siren howls anew, without the work in this shop suffering interruption. Suddenly, violent roaring and rumbling in a corner of the hall at the opposite end from ours; clouds of steam rise up with an almost unbearable hissing and a machine starts up whose insufficiently oiled bearings screech so loudly that one has to cover one's ears, whether one wants to or not. These are new turbines, as I learn in a quieter interval, which are connected to a steam pipe on the test stand. There can be no thought of sitting down, of resting. I am scarcely granted the most indispensable breaks. I am sent from one machine to another, am lent out, am charged with all the little errands outstanding, as if it has been tacitly agreed that I should not catch my breath for a moment. (A test?) At last as the afternoon draws on, I lose the feeling of tiredness. I care about nothing. I move in the direction I am pushed, I do what I am told, I do not think clearly at all any more, it's only luck that I am not caught by a machine and dragged into an unguarded gearbox mechanism. Finally, I remain for most of the time at the foot of "my" crane; to say "my" is untrue, since I belong just as much to all the other crane drivers and charge hands. I am no longer aware of my limbs, my body stops short at my wrists, which I still feel as painful and swollen. Yet I am standing idle, while all around me work is going on with undiminished intensity. I see how the blade wheel of a turbine is made, how the plough-like steel parts are wedged on to the main shaft one piece at a time, while by means of a special method of measurement the tester lying on the floor registers deviations of a fraction of a millimetre. For even an inaccuracy of a tenth of a millimetre has the most terrible consequences given the furious speed of the machine when it is in operation. Even when the machine is running properly, one can feel the hurricane-like rising and swelling storm of air in the hall; the whole, solidly built edifice with its iron girders shakes on its foundations. The crude steel comes from one side, the materials side, there it is worked on; semi-circular bars are first of all dressed at high temperature, then milled as free of vibration as possible, then drawn, then processed further by the cube-shaped semi-automatic lathes. Every possible stage of this happens simultaneously, changes position, is lifted, put down, replaced, fetched, nothing is forgotten in the jumble of iron, of active, working and passive, processed metal, everything has its place and its purpose. I am the only one who is straying unthinkingly around here, now no longer even understanding the signals the crane driver gives me, sometimes come uncalled and another time let him wait, it is as if I am dazed, blocked. This state is also familiar in overworked horses, a stage at which they are altogether skittish, accept everything and nothing, and at this stage they are unpredictable, are then to be approached only with the greatest caution. No caution is necessary with me. It is as if I am under the influence of strong alcoholic drinks, without desires, almost insensible. I pull myself together, stand up straight, just as far as my normally gawky posture allows. To look at there is nothing out of the ordinary about me except a certain mechanical, foolish smile, accompanied by an equally mechanical movement of my oil-covered hands, which I draw across my face the back of my head, whereby I only increase the itching and impregnate skin and hair even more thoroughly with iron and coal.

Our work lasts the longest since we have to pass on by crane a number of workpieces which are "finished", made ready by the others. Finally this work, which I can no longer properly follow, is also at an end. I stagger through the suddenly deserted machine shop, after my left foot almost tripped on a rung of the ladder. The hall is now quite abandoned, enlivened only by cleaners; the machines stand still. The next shift does not arrive till later. Now one comprehends the immense size of the building.

I make my way to the changing room of the newly equipped factory, where rows of naked workers are washing themselves under cold showers. Very young, porcelain-like, hard and whiteish bodies, almost entirely hairless are to be seen, and those which are entirely covered with thick brown hair, others, whose dark heads and body hair are already mixed with grey, often still display the most magnificent muscles. All of them stand there with bent backs, the part of the body upon which they allow the water to fall especially abundantly. I too have the greatest longing for water, I hurry towards it, but am knocked aside by another troop crowding in and now lie on the floor. The clean water and also some of the dirty water runs on to my face, into my ears. I see on the clean, slippery floor, made up of tiny stones, hard by my mouth, the feet of the workers' wooden-soled clogs. A single second lying there is sufficient to shake off all fatigue, to come to myself again. I rise with an attempt at a laugh. I energetically push my way in, shower amply, then dress as quickly as possible. I leave the changing room, I am at the next moment, without noticing how, in the street, in the next but one already far away from the sphere of the turbine factory.

There are broad boulevards, the railway station is near, but I hardly recognise it again, it does not seem to be the same one as yesterday. I make for home, to "my" lodging house, but do not reach it. I collapse on a bench, which belongs to the gardens of a public park (did I not in Onder-kuhle once dream of a ride in this park . . . with my father . . . on Cyrus? . . .), look around observantly just once more, as if to feign posture and consciousness, and am at the next moment sunk in an unnaturally sudden, nightmare like sleep, from which I am only woken by the hand of a policeman. It is midnight. The policeman does not believe me to be a vagrant, rather he fears that my few possessions could be stolen while I am sleeping. For that reason he woke me, after, as he tells me, he observed me for an hour.

5

The days pass at a furious pace. I must look for other, cheaper lodgings, but during the first week cannot find the time to do so.

On Saturday the occasion of receiving wages has a certain degree of solemnity. Naturally I am tired on this day too, although I have only worked five hours instead of the usual nine. Nevertheless my posture (now that it no longer matters), is better than on the day I received my report in Onderkuhle. Not a trace any more of awkward and clumsy bearing. I do not care who is standing near me and could perhaps make fun of me at the mention of my aristocratic name. Besides no one does so, each person is concerned with himself and is only waiting for the money, in order to leave the factory as quickly as possible. The ceremony, does not last long. The wages lie in oblong, wheat coloured envelopes, counted out to the last coin for every name. No receipt, no scribbling. The checking must take place on the spot, complaints must be made immediately, not to the disbursing clerk, but to another one. Since the names are often identical, a job title is added, such as fitter, driver, electrician, draughtsman, pattern maker, winder, welder, riveter, foundryman, smith, milling machine operator, piece marker, checker, blade turner, joiner, mechanic, furnace man etc. Part of my money I immediately take to the post office, in order to pay off part of my debt to the shopkeeper in V., then I proceed to look for lodgings and rent the very first room, which, as I later discover, is too expensive, in view of what is being provided. It is no mere place to sleep, but a separate room belonging solely to me, in a six storey tenement with four staircases, which are all very busy and (at least today, on the general cleaning day), are fairly clean, the whole inhabited by countless small households. On moving into the room, I look forward to the next day, I should like to go to mass in the cathedral, which my parents have attended regularly for years, and request my landlord, a Jewish tailor with a large family, to have me wakened punctually. Remarkably I only wake towards evening on Sunday. Despite my healthy appetite and without answering the landlady's countless attempts, even if only by turning over in bed, I had almost completely slept through the day of rest. I step out on to the street, walk a few steps and then go into a cinema, since I have an urge to spend the Sunday at recreation just as unthinkingly as I spend the week at work.

The rest of the audience in the small cheap cinema also consists almost entirely of workers, male and female. When I am asked the next day how I spent the Sunday, and in embarrassment I say nothing, I am invited to join a workers' sport association, in which football is played and which is said to have an excellent team. That would at least offer a possibility of not being consumed by the completely exhausting work, which uses up every last portion of spiritual and mental strength. Just as soon as, for certain reasons, it becomes possible for me, I shall certainly do it. Who woke me on the following Sunday, I do not know. But I got up, just in time not to miss the hour of high mass in the famous cathedral. I drink up my coffee without sitting down, buttoning up my clothes at the same time, I take the bread with me. Thus I do manage to leave a little earlier and hurry towards the house of God.

I see the streets empty now on Sunday morning. The cabs wait at the stands, in front of the old wrecks with their flaking varnish and faded upholstery doze the nags, tired, overworked, never properly rested, with their crooked front legs, their thin drawn-up back legs, bony haunches, scrawny necks, which are only scantily framed by unkempt, never properly curried manes. The horses' lips droop as much as their eyelids. They stand there nodding, and the coachman on the seat dozes away just like them in the heavy, hazy, warm summer air. A horse with a conspicuously dejected expression, its eyes watering from old age, especially arouses my sympathy. I cannot refrain from pushing my breakfast roll between the mare's long, green stained, probably never polished teeth. The animal almost takes fright at the unexpected gift. Then she grinds hurriedly, making the chin-strap creak and the little chain rattle, she gobbles greedily, stares at me, taps the ground with a comprehending, intelligent motion of the long, irregularly shaped head. She then opens her mouth to whinny wistfully and hopefully and with such volume, that the ice grey, but red-cheeked, healthy, fat coachman awakes cursing and boxes the animal's ears with the whip handle. She falls silent at once, only turns her strangely shaped head towards me, as I quickly hurry away. I have always loved animals and, I admit it, not always loved without a feeling of envy. For the first time there is today also much pity.

Now I have arrived at the giant cathedral door. Mass has not yet begun, the majority of churchgoers are only just coming. I expect to see my parents. No couple that matches them. Suddenly I see a lady who is dressed with very fine, if also already somewhat old-fashioned elegance, wears many black beads on the crinkled taffeta of her dress and iridescent ostrich feathers on the wide and gently curved hat. The lady who, with head lowered, now steps through the door, with one hand gives the beggar something, with the other reaches out to the holy water font, is my mother. I do not understand this sight. I cannot grasp that my father is absent! But my thoughts are already being drowned out by the booming of the organ with its two hundred stops, which is the glory of this church . . . How different this house of God, how different the little college chapel in Onderkuhle, on to whose steps the high-spirited birds from the nearby poultry yard were always straying. There the divine service was no more than a kind of religious study period, during which the self-evident, that is, the undiluted Catholic faith, was made clear to us, practically and with a little solemnity – in addition there was a reminder of the doctrine of redemption, prayers for the health of the royal dynasty, then for the happiness of our parents, our benefactors, prayers for the salvation of the dead, finally prayers for ourselves, which after an appropriate interval took last place. Here, however, tremendous pomp, an overwhelming crowd of people, the vestments of priests and assistants of such magnificence, that the precious stones embroidered on surplice and dalmatic are blinding. Music of enchanting sweetness, crushing strength: boys' choirs, choirs of women's voices, the solo by an opera singer, the Latin mass, clouds of incense, the silvery ringing of the little bells, the utter silence during the sacrament . . . all unfamiliar, overpowering and oppressive like the first day in the turbine factory . . .

I look for refuge with my mother. At last I discover her in the semi-darkness in the usual place, where our pew is situated. But the ostrich feather hat hides her features from me. Now she raises her head. Does she feel my gaze? She seems to breathe more effortfully, and her pretty cheeks, which have become somewhat fuller, seem to tremble and grow pale in the uncertain light. Does she sense that her only child embraces her with his shy glances? It is impossible to tell. I feel her to be far away. I pray for my father, for my mother, perhaps I also pray for myself.

The absence of my much loved father grieves me greatly. Not that I could have demanded it. But the disappointment is too sharp, and, more than that, there must be an extraordinarily serious reason for his absence. I cannot explain why he, for whom piety is a matter of the heart, is missing on such a day. I pray without stopping.

Whether I still possess all the strength, with which I could once pray as a child, I do not know. Can someone be weak in faith (how much! how much!) and yet strong in prayer? Unanswerable question. If a man can draw comfort from prayer, then he needs no other. Only because my father possessed this comfort, could he sleep peacefully, whereas I, his son weak in faith, lying awake on the crescent shaped settee, felt myself drop down into the endlessness of the world, which opened up beneath my feet.

I bless him now, my father, I also bless my mother, I pray, as well as I can, for the survivors of Onderkuhle, for the animals there, Cyrus above all, also for the Master, for Titurel, I pray too for my work, which I now carry out in the factory and which awaits me tomorrow. The great power of the music, the proximity of the devout people, the mystery of our mass – and the worry about my father have in the end after all taken me out of myself, and so I leave the church with the "ite, missa est", comforted and exalted together with almost a thousand people. I no longer see my mother.

I must absolutely find a way, without interruption to my wearisomely begun work, to call on my parents. Now, I feel, it is possible to do so. Not today. Today I am too anxious, not quite equal to bad news. But tomorrow certainly or in the days that follow.

Outside it has begun to rain, and the air smells sweetly of trees in bloom. The acacias are blooming very late this year, only now, in July.

6

The following Tuesday, to my great astonishment, I find a
notice from the post office that I should present myself to
take receipt of a communication. This is almost impossible
for me, since the counter opening times are organised in
such a way that I must either forego my principal meal when
I come from the factory exhausted, or leave the communication lying there unclaimed until Saturday afternoon. Suddenly I wonder whether I could not take the night shift?
The night work cannot be any harder than the work by day,
but presumably it is better paid, I can then above all visit
my parents, without waiting until the end of the new week
to do so. I am very unsettled, I do not for a single minute
stop worrying about them. I volunteer on Wednesday morning, and my request is gladly satisfied. On Thursday morning
too, admittedly, I awake as usual at five o'clock, but go
walking until eight, then collect the communication from
the post office. It is the sum of money which I sent off to
V. the previous Saturday to pay my debts. Debit balance
settled! it says on the counterfoil of the remittance. Does
that mean that my debt has been paid by someone else?
Then it can only have been the Master, who even now did
not want to permit one of the pupils of Onderkuhle to

contract debts with a stranger. I resent this conduct, although it presumably arises from good intentions. But I no longer want to be under the sway of Onderkuhle, I want to do what *I* must and what *I* want, for that is one and the same. But with these thoughts I only partially dull the gnawing anxiety about my father. I think of bringing him flowers, but then I persuade myself that he is healthy, how ridiculous I would be then, if I arrived with a bunch of flowers! I feel that I must see him, that I cannot wait an hour longer. Perhaps it is enough, if I only see him, perhaps he will not ask me any question, perhaps I can keep silent about what happened in Onderkuhle and which profession I have taken up here. Onderkuhle is done with. Have I sunk? Have I risen? No matter – I must go to him.

In great haste I stride through the streets, which today especially have the radiance of early summer, everything shines, everything is healthy, solid and bright. I am aware of my youth, my strength which cannot be broken even by the heavy work.

But I no longer hunger for "tests". I am in reality.

If only my father is healthy! I pull the bell of our apartment. The very familiar, almost barking peal, unforgotten during my seven year absence, rings out. It takes less than three heartbeats, before my mother flies to the door, first of all fumbles nervously opening the patent lock, and then flings open the door in front of me. She beams at me with her short-sighted, light brown doe eyes; just awakened from sleep (the second time she dropped off, I learn later), she embraces me with her warm, tender arms, presses me to her, kisses me, who is a head taller. To a stranger (but there is complete silence in the big apartment), to a stranger it might appear that we are entwined heart to heart and that only my clumsiness and timidity prevents our lips from touching. I know, however, that she avoids physical contact even with her son. I know that, for all her love, *she* cannot overcome her peculiarities or inherited antipathies. But this mother's kiss will not be lacking. If only my father is healthy and without cares! The cares I want to take upon myself and can do so; but how provide him with fresh health? My mother looks so unconcerned, she draws me into her room like a high-spirited boarding school girl. But why does she not lead me to my father? Why no word of him? "I am sleeping in the boudoir now," she says, "in eight rooms we" (*We*, the word does me good), "in eight rooms we have put down moth powder and drawn the curtains, until we have a replacement . . ." So nothing need be lost yet, otherwise she could not have made her arrangements with such peace of mind. But why does she not speak of him? Around her lips there is sometimes a forced smile, her delicate brown eyelids are somewhat creased and their trembling often extends into the beautiful, dark blue eyelashes. I step into the boudoir. It does not look untidy, but also just as little put in order. Perhaps to save herself the trouble of bed-making, she has made up a bed of blankets and silk pillows on an old-fashioned couchette, where she sleeps at night, presumably also rests during the day. Beside it stands an old-fashioned standard lamp, by whose light she probably spends half the night reading. Numerous books are scattered across a fur-trimmed blanket, once a coach or sleigh blanket; on a little corner table, which serves as a repository for all manner of toilet articles, also stands her old, little carved ivory crucifix in a pale blue, silk-lined case. Before this kneels one of the countless dolls which my mother owns. There are dolls in every corner of the room, large and small, babies and peasant women, dancers and chimney sweeps all mixed up. Some with open, some with closed eyes, one is wearing a gold thimble (I remember, it was a Christmas present from my father in one of the "better" years of my childhood – I too received a present then), a golden thimble pressed on to the tiny little head, another, of giant size in comparison, has the famous pearl collar, made up of pearls of different colours, wound round its neck and around its wasp-like, laced-up doll's waist. My mother throws the whole company of dolls into a heap, but for all her impetuousness takes care that literally not a hair on the head of a single doll comes to harm. At the same time she is overflowing with the most impulsive tenderness towards me, she takes me playfully in her arms as if I too was an oversized doll, pushes me away again, in order to see me better from a certain distance, she talks without stopping, giving me no time to reply. She had already recognised me by the ringing at the door, she is so happy to see me. "I must take a closer look at you dearest, yes, it's a miracle! And your beautiful hair!" she says. As she looks out of the window, I hear the bell of the milk-cart. "Now at last it's the man with the cream," she says, "I thought before when it rang, it was him, usually he always comes earlier. We now must make do without a servant, the caretakers' wife helps now and then, she does not have much time, is expensive, I think, but it will not be long now . . . it will not be long now . . ." She repeats this phrase mechanically, her thoughts somewhere quite different again, probably with my poor father, then she pulls herself together: "We posted it up at the club, someone must present himself today, a new servant, someone whom your father likes . . . Ah, how did you, great big sweet boy, spend the night?" she asks further. "Oh, the terrible accident! Onderkuhle in flames! And I never saw it! But they are rebuilding it, besides it makes no difference at all, you are not going back to that place any more, after all, dear big boy! I never liked it. Your father wanted it. But I did not like it at all. Now I have you here again! Sweet thing! The Holy Mother of God has brought you back to me! It was your birthday too only a few days ago! How old are you? No, don't say anything. I am growing old, nothing but grey hair . . . Oh, that he is no longer with us, our good old David! It is indeed true that towards the end he rarely washed, and if we had company, we had to take a hired servant and, of course, also a cook and scullery maid, but in the past year that was only once. Now I shall fetch the cream; no, I believe the caretaker's wife is taking it from him downstairs, he must not walk on the stair carpet, the uncouth milkman, it will soon be nine, she usually comes at this time, the stupid woman . . ."

"How is my father?" I ask.

"I am anxious about him," she says. How much, is demonstrated to me by the suddenly darkening gaze and the movement of her lips, which admittedly are still completely smooth and unwrinkled, as if painted with enamel, but now assume a stubborn and deeply despondent expression.

"Why is that? What is wrong with him? Is he seriously ill? Who is treating him? For how long? Why was I not told long ago?" I ask.

"He is still sleeping," she replies, with a strange emphasis on these words.

"Still? Why?"

"Only recently. Every day, he believed you were coming. He very much wants to see you. He awakened always at about seven o'clock, so also today. He wants to keep his eyes open. He even forces himself to go to the bathroom and shave off his beard. Then he wants to receive you. But he cannot. When the milkman rings at nine o'clock, papa strangely is lying fast asleep, and nothing wakes him before midday."

"Is it weakness? Is he in pain?"

"Do I know that? I do not know. Come into the room, my beloved. I did not want to write anything unpleasant. Is that not proper? Perhaps he can hear us, so careful! Now, however, I must tell you everything . . ."

I look at my mother, but she does not look at me. There is complete silence, in which can be heard from time to time, perhaps because the wind carries the noise closer, the wheezing breath of my father, which is a little reminiscent of the whirring of the Jewish master tailor's sewing machine. I must not think of my father's end! Now my mother briskly tidies up, which means, she gathers up the volumes of novels, piles them one on top of the other, the open pages facing upwards. In among them there is also her gilt edged breviary. The dolls form another heap. She makes herself beautiful, a few dabs with the powder puff, then the hairpins taken out, the still full hair combed through with a wide-toothed comb: "Do not look at me, my boy, I beg you!"

I can no longer feel my heart beating, I am beside myself with fear . . .

Her toilet, so casually begun, appears to have become protracted.

I ask once again, "What is happening? You wanted to tell me something else?"

"I? Tell you? No, I don't remember, darling. Say, do you want to breakfast now? Have you already taken a bath today? I take a bath every morning at five. Then sleep a little more, that does me good, but then I don't shut my eyes until two o'clock in the morning, no, one o'clock, or even midnight . . . But tell me, do you not want to see papa then?"

Without replying, I nod. She leads me to him. The curtains are open, swaying back and forward in the morning wind. The air is fresh and cool. My father is lying in bed. The illness must have altered his face completely. It is he, and yet now he is like a very old, very unfamiliar man, sunk deep in sleep. Not a hair on the faintly shining crown, only a scanty snow-white fringe at the back of his head and a tuft behind each ear. The mouth very soft, the lower lip drooping, coloured a dull blueish red. Above it a very fine, white, crescent shaped moustache, which covers the sensitive upper lip; as if woven of silken threads, it quivers with every breath. A silent figure, sunk deep into itself. The eyes closed, hidden behind tea rose coloured eyelids, their curvature is somewhat flattened, hardly arching up at all out of the depths of the dark rimmed eye sockets. The upper part of the sleeper's body has been leant upright against the pillows in a dignified but very uncomfortable position, which is very taxing for the heart, as is evident from the parchment-like pallor of the deeply lined cheeks. To my mother's great astonishment I remove the uncomfortable pillows, and the long cool head sinks as if lifeless, rustling softly, on to my sleeve. I lift the blanket. I grasp his feet. They are, like the curved feet of the ivory crucifix in my mother's boudoir, yellow, cold, noble, motionless. They are not the caricature, but the image of his hands, which even now, bathed in the full light of the July sun streaming in, lie folded on the rust red blanket, just as I put them down after I first kissed them . . . I should like not only to kiss his hand, but to embrace him, call him, say that I am here, be with him, remain! To remain with him, appears to me now as better, more worthwhile than anything else. But how to disturb the death-like sleep? Can I do it? May I do it? Must I do it?

My mother has watched impatiently. Now she pulls both my hands away, squeezes them between her warm, satin soft hands: "Let him sleep, dear heart!"

"But can it go on like this? . . . He does not have much strength to lose . . ."

"I said exactly the same yesterday to the caretaker's wife. In the same words . . ."

"What is to be done? What does the doctor order?"

"The family doctor has become somewhat uneasy. But he thinks that it is anaemia and vascular deficiency . . ."

"Does he know his job? Do you have confidence in him?"

"If I were sick myself, certainly . . ."

"Shall I get another doctor? What is the name of the chief physician to the Royal Household?"

"Yes, do you really think it is serious? Yesterday papa was anxious, he also spoke yesterday of Professor B. But how should we get to him? It is so difficult to reach him . . . I have so much to do at home . . . There are others coming too. Today papa wanted to talk to his notary . . . The abbé is also seeing to him . . ."

I no longer hear the last words. I plunge down the stairs, past the astonished wife of the caretaker, look up Dr B's apartment in an address book in the nearest shop, take a carriage, urge the coachman to make haste, learn at the doctor's magnificent, quiet house that he no longer lives here, but has built himself a villa in a suburb, is, however, hardly to be reached there now either, but at the university hospital. I drive there, with the greatest difficulty get past the reluctant staff to the professor, who, however, for some reason is friendly and obliging, excuses my importunity with a courteous smile and promises to come in the afternoon. I immediately hurry back home.

I have been away for little more than an hour, yet I find the house completely altered. The doors are wide open, there is a smell of medicine and incense, hats hang on the pegs in the dreary passageway with the huge but empty closets. The ancient family doctor leaves the sick room, reaches for his fine panama hat, catches sight of me, recognises me, wants to say something, but thinks better of it, merely runs the back of his hand quickly along the bright tartan hat band and leaves the house, but nevertheless calls from the open front door, "I'm coming back. I'm fetching a preparation. I'll be back soon." I now hear my father conversing in a low voice. My mother comes towards me, carefully dressed, wearing a little perfume, but with eyes lowered, dejected. "He is coming, the professor is coming," I whisper to her. "Thank God!" she answers with a sigh, but turns again to the caretaker's wife and gives her instructions for lunch. Then to me again: "Go to him now, but do not forget, what you promised me . . ."

7

I enter. Only now do I really see my father. When he becomes aware of me a pale flush crosses his face, beads of sweat appear on his bare high forehead, and his mouth begins to laugh, the delicate white moustache trembles. Beside him, on the beautiful tapestry chair, sits the notary, there is a document on his knees and a portable inkwell, such as the students in hospital use, is close to hand. Now he stands his pen holder upright, so that he does not bespatter the document, and looks at me expectantly, if also somewhat impatient at the interruption. At the same time our old father confessor (my first teacher of reading and writing) enters quietly. He blesses me with his wonderfully gracious, swinging movements, as if he were fanning me. My father is silent. He is speechless with joy. He kisses me firmly on the mouth. His cheeks, which nestle against mine, are smooth. His lips are warm, full, alive. And now that he has come as close to me as is possible, I can see that, for all his joy, his eyes shine with the calm, blue brightness which has always attracted me. I am one with him, I never want to be without him again . . . I do not want to believe that it is serious, I will not have it, it must not be. But against my will, my mouth tightens into a distressed expression. The old man passes his outspread left hand over my whole face in order to smooth it out. Then he raises me, with a mere glance, from my knees, introduces me to the notary, who, a head smaller than I and thin as a walking stick, firmly shakes my hand. Then he sits down again and waits. The abbé, who has evidently already completed his duties here today, takes his leave.

My father points me to a seat and continues his conversation with the notary. He is a little embarrassed, but nevertheless does not send me out of the room. For his departure, he searches his mind for goods and gifts, in order to assign them. But there are no riches to bequeath. I also no longer see in the corner the old cuirass, which in years gone by he wanted to leave to the Municipal Museum; in the glass case there were once precious objects, now no longer; the golden spurs rested on white satin cushions, now the place is empty, and the midday sun is refracted in the mirrors which form the back of the glass case. My father has perhaps nothing to leave behind, but for his name and his ring. He has no task which has to be continued, no instructions to give on the further guidance of an enterprise, as has, for example, the owner or managing director of a big turbine factory. The only thing which would have been left to him would have been my education. He loved my mother, but he preferred to have me educated by Onderkuhle rather than by her. But did he not know, that *he* was the only one for me? Everything, life and death, vocation in earthly life, infinity in the future one, the absolute immeasurability of the individual and his despair, everything lay in *his* hands, which he now spreads out empty in the noonday light, the pale red, very lined, somewhat damp palms facing upwards. How different my youth would have been with him! Can it be over? Not the length of a year with him? A short time ago Onderkuhle came to an end, the ashes there are still warm – and now this one and only man shall be lost to me?

The notary does not have much more to write. There follows a short clause about the pension from Ireland and its employment, for as long as my mother is alive and for the time afterwards. My thoughts on that are quite different, but I am silent, and do not interrupt my father's last wish. The notary rises. He goes.

My mother enters with a tray, but my father touches only just enough of each course so that he can praise my mother for the excellent preparation. She then beams at the flattering words, which she does not quite deserve. Then she leaves us alone.

My father looks at me for a long time and then says, "Please, assist me, I wish to get up." I obey him silently, hand him the necessary pieces of clothing, support, when needful, his back, under his arms and help him to the tapestry chair. He breathes deeply, is paler rather than more flushed with the exertion, has become quieter rather than more animated, and merely squeezes my hand with a long, firmly encompassing grip and says nothing. The doorbell rings, someone enters the hallway on tiptoe and talks to my mother in a low voice. My father turns to me: "How are you living?"

"I am working in a turbine factory."

"So. Are you contented?"

"Yes, I am contented."

"I know the company, fifteen years ago I was offered a position on the board, I declined, since it is repugnant to us to receive money without rendering service, and my contribution would have been practically nil."

When I protest, he says, "Yes, I know it is so. Perhaps I was not right. I should have been able to do more for you both. Are you contented now?" he repeats.

"Yes, certainly," I say, "if I am with you."

"Not in that way, as you well know; not in that way, I do not wish it."

"I am contented."

"I am glad. That comforts me greatly. I am very glad."

The final words only emerge laboriously and very slowly from his ever paler mouth. Is he fading? I want to speak with him, as I look at his noble, oval, already azure blue finger nails, I want to address to him the nonsensical plea which all survivors address to the dying, that they should not leave after all, that for our sake they should not do it. But I maintain my composure. I do not weep. Tears never came easily to me. I press my lips together and stifle every outburst of emotion. After a short oppressive interval, the old family doctor enters. Evidently he has brought my mother gloomy information. She follows close on his heels, almost pushes me aside, holds the old doctor by the arm and threatens not to let him go, until he has saved my father. She insists on another examination and in her agitation employs words of whose significance she is not aware. The old doctor gives way to her urging, and we, the doctor and I, unclothe my poor father, who puts up with everything and even soothes my mother who is trembling with rage. All the pieces of clothing which, with my help, he so laboriously put on, are pulled off. At last he lies there almost completely unclothed. What a son feels at the sight of his almost naked father cannot be described. But I control myself, my father does so too. What is the point of this terrible activity? What can one hear from this heart? What can one feel in this body? First of all the old doctor, whose own life is already drawing to a close, orders silence, although we are not making the slightest movement, then he examines, presses and kneads the delicate patient, who, however, does not flinch, in this too revealing himself as a former pupil of Onderkuhle, then the doctor raises his eyes to the ceiling, as if the answer were written there. Finally the family doctor shrugs his shoulders and in a somewhat shaky voice refers us to the "modern" viewpoint of the professor, whom we are all expecting. My mother covers father with a faded, copper coloured silk blanket and supports his lean, yellow head, which is ready to sleep again, with so many heavy pillows, as if he were already to be laid out now. The prince composes himself, on his face appears an expression of energy which is very rare in him, but for that reason unforgettable to me, he wants to speak, still tell me much. Then as he is still silently moving his lips, sleep, approaching death, overwhelms him. My father squeezes my hand almost painfully, as if his body wants to ask me to wake him, when the soul is already sleeping. But no son does that.

My mother weeps, or more accurately, she pours forth tears, which flow from her beautiful pale brown eyes without any effort. The ancient family doctor is embarrassed, rubs his plump, reddish hands and orders calm, as if my father were not overabundantly blessed with it already . . .

8

The surgeon does not appear as promised at five o'clock, but not until about eight o'clock. It has meanwhile become almost unbearably sultry, and a storm of thunder, lightning and hail bursts from sulphurous yellow clouds as the doctor, a thick-set gentleman with a double chin and chubby dark red cheeks, enters, smelling strongly of lysol and lily of the valley. First the doctor solemnly removes his hat and his gloves, he takes up position in front of the patient, trying to hide his fat chin by gravely throwing back his head, as if he were a horse that with head held high had to demonstrate the art of equestrianism. After he has, as he believes, made a sufficient impression on us, he bends down to the patient. His fixed expression dissolves, he examines my sleeping father, who is not to be woken by rough shaking, with his padded fingertips, then draws down the lower left eyelid, to check the content of the blood by the colour, thoughtfully pushes the sparse hair at the ears back into place, then in conclusion nods to himself, carefully covers Father up again and turns away. An operation would be possible, he says. "Would it promise to be a success?" we ask with one voice. "The promise is certainly made, but is seldom kept," he replies with dry doctor's wit. Can we not at least count on a renewed improvement, I ask. My mother swallows her sobs, her pearl-like little teeth bite into a lace-trimmed handkerchief. The doctor has already picked up his hat, his eyes wander over the shabby furnishings of the three-windowed drawing room transformed into an improvised sick-room, remembers the distinguished name, which is presumably familiar to him from court, then puts down his hat and comes back to the sick bed again. He drops down into the arm chair and thinks it over once more. "Naturally I could attempt the operation," he says finally, "but even in the case of a favourable outcome, the success will only be a temporary one. This process cannot be stopped. Whether his physical condition is good enough to withstand a lengthy and technically difficult operation, which would no doubt be a triumph of surgery, is also a problem. Is it not better, if we let the patient gently slumber away, spare him pain, as far as that is possible? That we can do." "Is there an immediate danger?" I ask, keeping control of myself with all the strength at my disposal. "Oh no, no danger, only a scientific necessity." "And how long?" "Diagnosis is the business of men, prediction the business of heaven. There is always room for illusions. Days or months, who knows . . . no one, not even he, whom it most concerns . . . and should not know it either . . ."

What else can we do but remain silent. The doctor glances through the clouded window-panes at the street, steaming after the rain. Then, so that something at least is done for him, he writes a few illegible characters with a fountain pen on a piece of paper and tells us to obtain the prescription. In this way he wants to provide the comfort that all help is not yet in vain, although only my mother lets herself be deceived, because she wants to be. I have had to deduce from the doctor's silence about his return, that he had no thought of doing so and that nothing more was to be expected. I am here calmly stating the facts. What I was feeling I cannot put into words.

One must keep to the tangible, as meagre, as insignificant, as desperate as that is. How can high ambition, passionate endeavour be possible for a young man, when he sees how little a man's life means to the world, the life of his father, which to him is the most important, the only important thing in his existence? However much he may grasp the world in its infinity as far as the unwalled spaces of eternity and the universe, he will still always only find support in his father; even national feeling is only father feeling. However much he may occupy himself with bitter necessity, with the struggle for a daily morsel of bread, he will still always only find peace and satisfaction with his father or with his off-spring. If there is anywhere in this unstable world support and true affinity, effortless understanding, true delight in people, living side by side without struggle and bitterness – what I longed for and never experienced with Titurel, then it would have been with my father. No room for illusions, as the clever professor says. He is only all too right. He is in the right with his doubting glance, which comprehends the whole shabby, emptied magnificence of our apartment, asking himself how these cheerless, bare rooms, in which no old piece of furniture is still serviceable, from which every serviceable new piece is equally missing, how these wretched, worn-out furnishings can be reconciled with our distin-guished name. Yes, we are the declining line, no one will need to reckon with us. But I have begun to reckon in the short time since Onderkuhle. I know what fee this professor can demand for his short visit, and I give him a somewhat higher sum. I very clearly see his astonished, but controlled smile. Even on the threshold he considers whether he should promise us the favour of his return. But he is honest enough to spare us the needless expense, himself the unnecessary journey and futile loss of time.

Can something be settled in such a way, that it is worth no further effort? "How old?" asks the doctor, still at the apartment door. When he has the age, he shrugs his heavy shoulders, as if to say: "Enough! Long enough!" Is it not better to take every last penny from a family of small means, but also to make every possible human effort to keep a life like this going? Only a month longer, a week longer, even the "temporary success", of which he spoke contemptuously, is it not much, must it not be everything for a son? How can someone, who has so many means at his disposal, descend the stairs on the runner and call out to us with bored lips, as he lights a cigarette: "Will hopefully soon be better again!"

We return to the sick room, look for the prescription, but in the twilight of the cloudy, sultry evening do not find it. We open the window wide. A strong, pure, almost palpable night thunderstorm air flows in, which is charged with magnetic force, and which no one, who still breathes, can resist. And what the efforts of the professor were unable to accomplish, this fragrant thunderstorm vapour can. The patient awakes, he feels no pain, his mind is clear, he revives in the truest meaning of the word. He now resembles once more the man who used to visit me in Onderkuhle. We talk again of days gone by and act as if it were still the good old days for all of us. We deceive one another, my father, my mother and I, we talk about what arrangements we want to make for the weeks of the "long vacation", we also briefly touch upon the project of the expedition to Central Africa with the Duke, which I hinted at to my father, and my father performs a little comedy with me for my mother. *He* knows how matters stand.

There are still clouds over the city, it is growing dark. The hour is approaching at which I am expected in the factory. If I did not come, in order to begin punctually, not much could happen to me. I could remain here, I could also, after the death of my father, have a share of the tiny pension (how tiny it is, I learned only today during the dictation of the clauses of the will) and so scrape by. My place in the factory would soon be filled, there is no gap to be closed. But something impels me there. I have the feeling, if I carry on a job, then I can trust in fate. The "world is, on the whole, benevolent" and it would not cheat me and let my father die while I perform the always identical manual operations in the factory, which every other hand could perform just as well. He too, whom it most concerns after me, seems to agree. Admittedly until now he has refrained from any judgement on my proletarian work, but this evening when I insist to my mother that I must meet friends from Onderkuhle in a bar, he smiles approvingly at me on parting.

As strange as it sounds, on this day I feel relieved for the first time entering the turbine hall at nine o'clock in the evening precisely. I believe that during the next nine hours nothing can happen to me except what is determined in the movement, the prescribed action of the machines around me. What am I during these nine hours? Very far from being the son of a prince, hardly even a man either. When one's hand is on the control levers, on the resistances of the electric motors, when with a push of the finger, without any further effort than is required to crush a fly, loads weighing many thousands of pounds are raised and lowered, one is part of the driving and of the driven machinery. Now I no longer have the delusion I as an individual am something which much be reckoned with and which fate has ordered into the endlessness of space and time, without giving this atom the strength to survive the fight, indeed not even the strength to consciously look this fight against death in the eye. At this moment the unnatural vitality of Onderkuhle no longer flows through me. The hour in the green riding school is not repeated. I live in reality, not roused higher, nor pressed lower. Something that is self-evident to many, but not an Orlamünde, makes me climb up and down the steps to the crane, give the iron chains an extra push, if they should be winding too sluggishly on to the cable drum, and in general do everything that is necessary to the noiseless performance of the dangerous work (much more dangerous for the workers below than for the crane drive and his assistants above). The machines, whose purpose and intelligence I now gradually begin to understand, as once the mechanics of the horse's paces during the advanced riding lessons, move without interruption and stoppage, thanks to a power which other workers in the power station a few kilometres away transmit to them. Our work too goes out into the world, it does not have its end here in the factory shop. We are machine tools of iron and some of us of flesh and blood and produce machine tools. I am now just as little afraid of coming to a standstill and of a fall into the abyss of the inescapable real, as a constellation is frightened of its motion and during this motion shivers with fear at this motion coming to an end. The fixed duration of this mechanised work is a comfort to me. I would have spent this day's terrible night after the doctor's visit in the awareness of the imminent and irrevocable end of the only person in the world whom I love, I would have spent this night more sorrowfully and full of desperation far away from the machines. Today I do not want to leave this station in life I have chosen for myself. If fate wills it, I shall for many years to come take my place beside this machine or beside another one of a similar kind, I shall always proceed to my place with my body, not with my soul, which is not included in the contract, at the same hour, with the same strength and the same will and shall leave it at the agreed time. No different from a planet, which enters the orbit of the larger and more steadfast constellations at the appointed hour and at the same appointed hour leaves this orbit. I shall no longer be Prince Orlamünde. What was he then anyway? What would he have become? Even the greatest of men does not lift the world off the hinges of necessity, as mortal body certainly never ever.

Perhaps I can live among people like myself. Now the crane driver can already understand me. He has chosen night work for a similar reason: because during the day he wants to visit his little daughter, the youngest of five, in the Park Hospital. There are visiting hours only on Wednesday, Saturday and Sunday. He very much wants to visit his daughter at least once a week and bring her trifles from home, since her mother is too much taken up with the other children. Also she is expecting a new addition to the family. Will I, with all my heart a son, one day be able also to assume the gravity of a father? My forebears had neither the courage to make an end, nor the courage to start from the beginning again. I shall not have one child, like my ancestors as far back as my great-grandparents, but either live childless or, if that is the way of it, I shall beget as many children as bread can be provided for them by my hard work. This plan too may appear self-evident to many, for me alone it has not been easy. Onderkuhle has no part in it, neither Cyrus nor Duke Ondermark, nor the Master, nor my only beloved friend Titurel. Not my father. Not my poor mother. That is over. The crane driver speaks of his apparently hopelessly sick child, I of my sick father, about whose prospects of recovery I am silent. I begin to operate the machine by myself. He gives me command after command with military precision, the simultaneous carrying out of two different movements causing me the most difficulties. Admittedly first of all I practise on the empty, unloaded crane and must learn to set all these levers and rings in motion automatically, before anything is entrusted to me in earnest. Yet a kind of delight in life fills me, when for the first time it works without a lot of squeaking and creaking of the machinery. (As a test, I lift the crane driver's parcel containing a doll for his child, a tiny load.) Delight in life at this simple and mindless work, which every reasonably skilled hand, every reasonably alert mind can do? Delight in life, with a sick father whom, after the end of the night shift, after I have bathed at home once again, I shall find, tomorrow at about seven o'clock, in the same lethargic, discouraging, even if not immediately threatening, condition in which I left him yesterday evening? But during the night he has at least emptied the glass of water, which I set down for him, has taken the new, wafer wrapped prescribed powder, his sleep is lighter, the dull parchment colour of his face has been replaced by a very delicate red. Has the professor after all been mistaken? Can I pray? – Yet also not despair. If I now lie down on the crescent shaped sofa, made up for me by the caretaker's wife acting as maid, with prickly velvet as sheet and worn out quilt as blanket and just before falling asleep stretch my limbs, massage the somewhat swollen wrist of my right hand and yet at the same time have to exercise the other wrist in order to gain some relief – then for the first time I experience what well deserved rest means and that even in my present life there can be benediction, not for all perhaps, but for my father's son, especially for him.

9

So the first days pass. Since my father's condition does not worsen, I am filled with great happiness, and wish only things may always remain thus, so modest have I become.

My mother has no objection to my going out every evening. Does she really believe I spend the nights in frivolous company, instead of keeping watch by my father's bed? It almost appears as if it is so. Again and again she puts the same question to me in the same words: whether I had enjoyed myself? And when I hand her a contribution to the housekeeping money, she wants to know whether I won the money at baccarat. I do not enlighten her. My real existence is a secret shared only by my father and myself, which he also never ever alludes to. The great deal of work in the still too extensive household is beginning to be an effort for my mother. Every day, candidates for the post of servant line up, who, however, each one for a different reason, do not meet with her approval, among them are also staff from House Onderkuhle, from whom I learn something of the fate of the Master, of the Colonel and of the Book-keeper. But my intercession on behalf of one of them, a young, very honest, even if not especially dexterous man (Fredy) is to no avail, my mother goes on looking, not thinking that the long wait is no help to my father, that he cannot look forward to countless months and years. In the meantime he must content himself with my care. My mother has the caretaker's wife fetch the food from a nearby restaurant. She displays a quite childish pleasure, because she can pick out the tastiest dishes from the very extensive menu. My father's alarming condition disturbs her pleasure as little as my need for quiet in the hours before noon. I usually come home about six, wait for my father's first awakening, feel his pulse, hear how he has slept, make up his bed again, then I go to rest and am soon lying in very deep sleep. Admittedly my work in the turbine factory even now, when I am allowed to work more independently, does not surpass the powers of an individual. But it is nevertheless not comparable to the work in Onderkuhle. Certainly there I sometimes had to strain my energies almost to breaking point, but that only occurred on occasional days. The motive was ambition and the desire to set new records in sport.

It is, however, something else, exhausting to quite a different degree, to carry on for weeks without a proper break, the same, even if only moderately difficult job for at least nine hours. Admittedly one can certainly perform such work without a particular expenditure of energy, but one must have one's rest, without rest it is ruinous. So if I am wakened around midday, my ability to work is put in question. But what then? I am now physically and mentally so bound to this mechanical work, that I cannot forgive my mother when she awakes me at an unsuitable time day after day. I admit, she means well. On one occasion I am supposed to look at a servant who is presenting himself, on another occasion to admire an especially beautiful passage in one of her novels, on another allow myself a little fresh air, take a little outing, usually it is only because she cannot manage the selections from the menu without me. She has her most charming smile on her firm, unwrinkled lips, she fans the drops of sweat from my face with the outspread menu, wants to wipe away the "bad lines". The pearl necklace clinks gently on her beautiful smooth neck as she does so. I check my anger, only give her a look which could tell her everything. But she does not take me any more seriously, says: "Big growler!" Does not ask as to the cause of my tiredness, which at this moment I might after all reveal to her. Then, however, I think better of it. The feeling of earning one's daily bread at eighteen years of age, and even if it is only with manual labour is so invigorating, so heartening, that I can bear much. Certainly there are hours, in which I too experience the bitter taste of this work, for in the factory I must not feel myself to be among equals. I well know a life in accordance with my rank, a carefree, hopeful life among people who are close to me by birth and education, is something different. But fate could be even harsher. Above all, I remain at the side of my old father, indeed, with inexhaustible joy I see in him a kind of recovery, a revival in spirit, a lessening of the pain, an awakening from the lethargy in which he lay until my coming. I cling to the professor's "months", of which until now only one has elapsed. I divide my time between essential rest and nursing him. He has begun to pull himself together, to actively resist his illness, he, who has never developed his will, now asserts himself against the illness, and he masters it in a manner which is quite admirable. There are perhaps men, death-defying explorers, people like Amundsen, heroes or priests, who sacrifice their life for their great cause. He, however, who long ago had already been entrusted to death, roused himself with all his manliness, solely to grant *me* for a while longer the blessing of his presence. One morning at the street corner nearest ours I meet a bent old man, wrapped in flapping grey garments, who totters towards me, leaning on his pale-coloured stick. I recognise this stick, which I already knew from my father when I was a boy, before I recognise him. In the morning, as my mother still slept, my father, gathering all his strength, dressed, came towards me and, since my return was delayed, waited a long time for me at the corner, half fainting from severe pains. To my deep sorrow I have to recognise that this effort was beyond his powers, today the happiness of once more walking through the streets beside him is a very bitter one, almost chokes my throat. On the first step, which leads from the mezzanine of our house to the first floor, his strength fails him completely, his head slides on to his chest, and I must support him, must take him, the light body with bones as weightless as bird bones, in my arms and carry him upstairs. From this day on begins his new decline, this time not to be checked by expenditure of energy. The family doctor finds everything quite natural, the recovery just as much as the deterioration. His smile drives me to greater despair than the professor's death sentence once did. My mother again has her inexplicable bursts of pain, which she then suffocates between the pages of her novels or in the tinsel embroidered skirts of her dolls, the abbé once again enters our house almost daily, and one morning, at my mother's request, gives my father the last rites.

I am a stranger to my mother, and she is a stranger to me. I do not love her, I cannot love her and shall not love her. I do what I can for her, I sometimes force myself to bring her small presents, to which she is very responsive. But more I cannot do. More is impossible. But do I not also demand the impossible of fate? Do I, not believing in miracles, nevertheless demand from fate the "small" miracle of restoring to an old man, who never harmed anyone, a few years of health?

And who deserves it more than he? If I look at him now and think that soon he will no longer be, then I do not know how I should bear that. If one should die, why not rather I? I cannot measure him by the same standard as other men. For me the whole of mankind consists of two parts, he is the one part, everything else is the rest. He is the most affectionate spouse, the most loyal, even if weakest father. Even now no word for or against my plan, and nothing more of the privations of one's station or of those willed by God.

Himself poor, he is a friend of the poor. Weighed down by his noble rank as if by a heavy armour, as almost listless offspring of a once powerful house, he did not want to bring his pound to market, to make the most of it. In his more than sixty years, he has acquired nothing and lost nothing. What remains after his death, will, thanks to the small pension from Ireland, be just sufficient to ensure for my mother the continuation of her present existence. I inherit nothing of it. I am my own master and therefore also my own heir – this he knows without words. He charges me to send back his orders "afterwards". They do not belong to him, are always only lent, never given away. One, the most important, goes back to the imperial government in Vienna, others to the royal house here. He has always avoided the various well-endowed honorary posts at court, the gilded Congo deals of the mercantile king. In return most of our equals in rank avoid us, only rarely does one of them enter our house. The Duke of Ondermark sent his secretary to obtain news about my father (and myself?). He did not encounter me. That was also more preferable to me. I was sleeping during this visit after an especially hard night at work. My father did not have me wakened and was right in that.

The only thing he has to bequeath, now that he feels his

end near, is his signet ring, which passes from generation to generation. Otherwise he wears no jewellery, not even an atom of gold on his person, neither a wedding ring nor a watch. For what do jewellery and time mean to this man? Now, on the 28th of August 1913, at two o'clock, he draws the ring from his left index finger, for the first and last time since my grandfather's death, and gives it to me. I want to refuse it, then, when this refusal is impossible, want to hide it in my pocket, but he says in a calm and composed voice, as if he is continuing a conversation begun long ago: "You wear it. Now it is your turn." Then he is silent. The afternoon passes as always. The priest comes, I leave the room. My mother has a fit of weeping, she suffocates it by pressing her face with all her strength against the light blue silk cover of her ivory Christ, so that then the folds of the silk appear imprinted on her round cheeks. Then she smoothes her reddened skin in front of the mirror for a long time. Without speaking I go into my father's room. The bells of the nearby church can be heard; later, from a more distant factory (not ours) a shrill siren. My mother, when I go to her, is sleeping exhausted, surrounded by all her dolls. I return to my father. "Do not weep!" he says to me after an hour. "How will you then be able to comfort your mother? I have confidence in you. May our Lord and Saviour continue to protect you." He looks at me and his left hand, which he has withdrawn from my face, hovers in a gentle circular motion through the big, shabby room. I cannot guess, and do not ask, whether he knows and approves of my *whole* existence, whether it distresses him that he leaves behind his son and wife in manifest poverty. He is very tired, the movement of his hand ends in a cursory yet solemn sign of the cross above my bright red hair, which his light hand only brushes. His strong, widely-spaced white teeth, which gleam vividly in his clay-coloured face pass over his drooping faded lower lip – then tiredness overpowers him. "I feel somewhat faint now," he says rather loudly, as if he was forcing himself to make this last effort, in order then to have the right to peace. "God and I are at peace. Always remain my son. God bless you! Take the pillows away from my head, lay them at my feet. You did that on the morning when you came from Onderkuhle. It was good. Good was it . . ." he says and with that sets the seal on his life, his illness, his love, his death. Without saying any more, he takes my right hand, with its scars from the fire at Onderkuhle, and the calluses from the turbine factory, in his left, holds it fast with a gentle pressure, then with the whole of his very light body he lays himself across my hands. He falls asleep imperceptibly.

Evening comes, night comes. My mother calls softly. I do not reply. She falls silent. I cannot get up, cannot move.

I cannot remove my hand from that of the dying man. It is an indescribable feeling, terrible and deeply moving, as I feel my right hand become lifeless, then, rising higher, my right arm and my shoulder lose all feeling and finally the whole right hand side of my body has fallen asleep, frozen and numb despite the sultry summer breeze, weaned of life and become a part of death with my dead father.

I can free myself the next day. It is a hot August day. My body lives and is strong and healthy as before. Only I am alone and shall remain so. I shall never again be afraid of death. No father of mine will die again. No man experience his own death.

On the evening of this day I go to the factory again, as I do not want to keep watch beside my mother. She is more composed than I. But even in her greatest distress she does not kiss me. This autumn she will already move to her cousin, the unmarried old Countess P. I shall remain behind alone.

But I shall not find the parting hard, for I shall live even more closely with my father, shall be absorbed even more by my work.

Ernst Weiss and 'The Aristocrat'

1

Ernst Weiss published more than a dozen novels, many stories and novellas, several plays and a considerable quantity of criticism and essays between 1913 and his death in 1940. Although he had enthusiastic admirers from the beginning of his literary career and his work was published by prestigious houses, major successes eluded him. After 1934, in exile in Paris and lacking a non-German readership, he lived in poverty. A few of his novels were republished in the 1950s and 1960s, and his last novel, *The Eyewitness*, was published for the first time. During these years, if Weiss appeared in the literary histories at all, it was as a minor character in the life of Franz Kafka.

The two appear to have become friends in 1913. Already resident in Berlin, Weiss acted as a go-between for Kafka during part of the latter's engagement to Felice Bauer. Weiss was present at the dramatic meeting in a Berlin hotel in July 1914 at which the engagement was broken off. He was critical of Kafka for resuming the engagement, which seems to have contributed to a cooling in the friendship.

Since the 1960s, Weiss has been rediscovered as a writer of lasting interest and this has played a part in a re-evaluation of the relationship between the two authors. 1982 was the centenary of Weiss's birth and was marked by the publication of the first collected edition of Weiss's work. By that year, one critic (Joachim Unseld) could describe Weiss as being a model for Kafka when the latter at last left Prague for Berlin in 1922 to live the life of a writer. (Kafka, of course, became fatally ill and died in June 1924.)

The friendship had never been completely broken. In the late 1930s, however, Weiss, although a sensitive reviewer of Kafka's work as it appeared in print, was still complaining in private that Kafka, whom everyone liked to regard as a saint, had behaved to him "like a scoundrel".

According to Margarita Pazi, the sense of injury which Weiss felt at being rejected by Kafka is reflected in *The Aristocrat*. In the novel, Titurel, humiliated, spurns his friend Boëtius, after the latter has saved him from drowning.

2

Weiss and Kafka came from similar backgrounds in the German-speaking Jewish minority (a minority within the German minority) of Bohemia and Moravia when these were still part of the Austrian Empire. Ernst Weiss's father was a textile merchant in Brünn (Brno) who died when his son was four. Weiss studied and practised medicine, as a surgeon, in Vienna, Berne and Berlin. After war service with the Austro-Hungarian forces, he gave up medicine to concentrate on writing, returning to Berlin where he remained until Hitler came to power in 1933. He died, as a consequence of attempting suicide, on 15 May 1940, one day after German troops entered Paris.

The novels and stories of Weiss and Kafka have certain common themes, notably a recurring problematisation of father-son relationships. And when, in 1937, Weiss reviewed Max Brod's biography of Kafka, writing of him as "a man . . . who truly could say of himself, it is a monstrous world he had in his head. It is not a comfortable friendly world," he could equally have been speaking of his own work. Nevertheless, for all the common aspects, which are also, in part, a measure of Kafka's influence on Weiss, they are very different as writers.

The Aristocrat demonstrates one obvious difference. Although the relation of father and son is the organising theme, it is the father's absence and weakness that presents a problem for the adolescent Boëtius von Orlamünde. He may feel powerless, but his father is not the unjust, oppressive, overwhelming presence of Kafka's stories.

If Kafka is careful and sober in style, then Weiss is breathless, almost careless. A desperate urge *to get everything in* sweeps the reader along and lends certain scenes in *The Aristocrat* an exceptionally dynamic quality with a quite physical impact.

This is above all true of a long scene in which Boëtius breaks in the stallion Cyrus. Yet the energy of the prose, the evocation of the effort and exhaustion of the protagonists, would be much weaker in its effect if Weiss was not also able to combine pace with the greatest precision in describing the equipment used and the responses of the horse.

This portrayal of bodies, human and animal, being tested, testing themselves to the utmost, has few equals. Occurring quite early in the book, although it follows briefer scenes of almost equal intensity, it takes the reader to the core of Weiss's novel.

The setting of the greater part of *The Aristocrat* is House

Onderkuhle, an exclusive boarding school for the sons of
the aristocracy. Onderkuhle is placed in eastern Belgium.
However, this is not much more than a half-hearted displacement, the author might just as well have written "somewhere
in the eastern territories of the Austrian Empire". The time:
a few months in the summer of 1913.

Boëtius von Orlamünde, a pupil at the school, is the only
offspring of an ancient but utterly impoverished noble family.
Eighteen years old and almost at the end of his schooling,
Boëtius no longer sees the point of the education he has
received. He has learned the acts of horsemanship and fencing. The most important subject at school, however, is the
forms of etiquette ("all the refinements of aristocratic
intercourse"). In the past, perhaps, these "forms" had given
structure and meaning to life; nobility was its own justification. Boëtius recognises the redundancy of his education,
yet he can conceive of no other standards by which to live
than those it instils. Unsure of a place in the world, receiving
no news from home, Boëtius more and more falls prey to
loneliness, dread, a fear of death. In the absence of guidance,
he searches out and accepts "tests", like the breaking in of
the stallion, which will justify his rank. However, they are
not enough. The horse's submission leaves him feeling disap-
pointed; the contest was unfair. Then, as the school burns
down and he is called on to display his courage by trying to
rescue a fellow pupil, he breaks down, fails to make the
attempt, finally (to himself) forfeiting his nobility.

Boëtius flees to Brussels, where his parents live, but finds
lodgings, and works as a labourer in a turbine factory. (The
manufacture of the engines is as powerfully captured in a
couple of chapters as the earlier struggle with the horse.)
Finally he does return to the parental home to be at the side
of his dying father.

The Aristocrat is presented in the first person in the guise of an autobiographical document written by Boëtius himself. With occasional lapses, however, the present tense is used, which lends immediacy. In other respects too, the notion of "reporting" is only loosely adhered to. The recounting of events flows into dreams and imaginings. The careful description of phenomena is frequently combined with the abandonment both of a coherent time sequence and of a fixed perspective. Boëtius often observes a single occurrence from more than one viewpoint, and the shift between them can take place several times within one paragraph. For example, when, on his return to Brussels, he hides in a doorway opposite his parents apartment, waiting for them to appear, his gaze is simultaneously on the entrance and inside the house.

At the conclusion of the novel, Boëtius seems reconciled to his fate. He appears to have renounced the role of aristocrat. After the seven years of separation in the boarding school, he was nevertheless at last granted his wish of being, for a few precious weeks, truly a son to his father.

The contemporary reader, however, knows just as well as did readers in 1928, when the novel was first published, that this cannot be the end of the story. Is it coincidence that Onderkuhle School, the stone repository of the old values, burns down on the 29th of June, 1913? That is almost one year to the day before the assassination of the Austrian crown prince, Archduke Franz Ferdinand, in Sarajevo. One year from the point in time at which the novel ends, its "hero" Boëtius von Orlamünde would have been a young officer, about to participate in the carnage of the Great War. There he would find a place, a purpose, in a new kind of army, just as he does in the army of labour in the turbine factory, whose work force is described as if it were a military unit. What kind of officer would he be? And, if he survived, what would he be likely to do afterwards?

3

Michael Hamburger (*A Proliferation of Prophets*, 1983), rightly recommends Ernst Weiss as one of the outstanding German novelists of his time, emphasising his "hectic imagination". Of *The Aristocrat* he concludes, "It seems unnecessary or irrelevant to state that [it] is a novel less about aristocracy . . . than about fear and the acceptance of death, about courage and cowardice, which Boëtius comes to see as 'more dangerous' than courage, about pride and humility, about nature and civilisation, about violence and tenderness. All these concerns are woven into a texture so seamless, that it becomes impertinent to pick them out."

While one can bear in mind the warning of that final sentence, it seems to me that such a summation of *The Aristocrat* renders it much more harmless, much more of a conventional *Bildungsroman* than it is. No place there for the perversity and misogyny of the hero and of other characters in the novel. Boëtius longs to be close to his friend Titurel, but it is, not least, the imperfections that are attractive. Boëtius' urge to dominate is quite evident. Visiting Titurel in the school hospital, he derives pleasure from the latter's weakness, from his rotten, decaying teeth, even from the smell that emanates from Titurel's mouth. He takes Titurel's hands, and they are like "warm meat".

Since being sent away to Onderkuhle School, Boëtius has

lived entirely in male society. His only contact with his parents has been occasional visits by and letters from his father. In the school, displays of weakness are grounds for punishment. When a young boy, Alma, bursts into tears during a swimming lesson, the most serious aspect of his behaviour is that he calls for his mother. "And after a few poor, feeble strokes the unbelievable happens: Alma loses his head, begins to cry for his mother . . . Naturally I pay no attention . . . Even in the greatest danger I would never have thought of my mother. I would never have called her. Only my father." The boy nearly drowns, and the Duke of Ondermark, a famous former pupil on a visit to the school, bursts into laughter.

The Duke is one of the two adults whom Boëtius considers as possible substitute fathers. The other is the school's Master of Ceremonies, who despite his low birth is the guardian of tradition, the teacher of etiquette. The Duke of Ondermark, however, with his *will* to command, and not simply an inherited right to do so, embodies a more modern form of leadership. But what kind of modernity does he represent? The expeditions, tightly disciplined, which the Duke organises for exploration in Africa, are machines designed for slaughter – of animals, of humans, it hardly matters which – and for the grabbing of booty. Boëtius admires the Duke because this field of action with its veneer of legitimation by science keeps him away from the embourgeoisement of the court (and the "Congo deals" of the King). Whether on one of his expeditions or attending a meeting of the Royal Geographical Society, the Duke remains in male society. His seeming modernity – exemplified by "the powerful, ear drum shattering Winchester rifles, such as have to be employed on hunts in the tropics" which have made him deaf on one side – involves paradoxically, a return to the oldest, the warrior justification of nobility. It is a nobility stripped of all the rather quixotic "gentlemanly" virtues maintained by Boëtius' father, who dies forgotten by court and society.

Boëtius may realise that the aristocratic ideal as taught at Onderkuhle is useless as a guide to living, but existence without the order of a rigid hierarchy is unimaginable. Indeed, order, knowing one's place, requiring distance, are so essential for him that he feels revulsion at unexpected contact with other – human – bodies. (Converted into "meat", like Titurel's hands, they become more bearable.) He complains that his mother has always flinched from kissing him, but the contradictory account of the reunion with her, after seven years, reveals that it is Boëtius who draws back from physical contact and projects this revulsion on to his mother.

It seems that, for Boëtius, affection is only possible within a hierarchical relationship (his love for his father) for example). Since he defines his father as his creator, the status of his "young mother" is problematic. She is excluded by the bond which unites father and son, is little more than a nuisance. As his father sinks away, Boëtius begins to hate her. It is she who should be dead. After the father's death, she is packed off to widowhood and poverty on a tiny pension, to live with the aged Countess P.

In truth, Boëtius feels closest to animals; beings who do not have the capacity for self-reflection on their condition. Enviable, he repeats several times. Though at one points he declares inanimate objects – stones – to be even more enviable. In the disciplined circumstance of the factory he approaches an ideal condition. "We are machine tools of iron and some of us of flesh and blood and produce machine tools."

Weiss's portrait of Boëtius von Orlamünde (and of Duke

Ondermark) is similar to the picture of "soldier males" that Klaus Theweleit, in *Male Fantasies* (1987 and 1989), derives from his reading of memoirs and novels by former members of the Freikorps, published in the 1920s and 1930s. (The Freikorps were armed bands of ex-officers and students who fought to defend "Germanness" in the Baltic states and on the eastern borders and put down working-class unrest in Germany itself.) Weiss, one guesses, shared some of the fears and obsessions of these displaced, unemployable and brutalised "White Guards" with their dangerous and absurd military codes of behaviour, whose only purpose in life was fighting.

For Theweleit, a key to understanding the proto-Fascism of the Freikorps men is their sense of being threatened by women, who do not fit into a very few firmly defined and subordinated categories. Something of Weiss's attitude to women can be gauged by the frequency with which the protagonists in his novels murder their wives. In *Georg Letham* the murder is carried out with a clinical lack of passion, almost in a spirit of scientific curiosity; in *Die Feuerprobe* (The Test of Fire) the murder instrument is a sharpened pencil (calling to mind the dispatch of female victims in Michael Powell's film *Peeping Tom*). In *Die Feuerprobe*, the narrator looks down at his apparently dying wife: "Now in pain the beloved face is distorted into any ugly grin. The mouth is a wide, bright red, wet pit, elongated, and the lips round about this pit are grey as her teeth." In much of Weiss's work there is as little mercy for the female characters as in a gallery of portraits by Edvard Munch.

Yet, of course, there is obviously no identity between Weiss and Boëtius von Orlamünde. However, the strength of the book, aside from its masterly depiction of an obsessive and acute awareness of the body, lies in its sympathy for a figure, who far from becoming more mature in the course of his adolescence, feels quite incomplete unless he can submit to a discipline, a leader. It is a figure whose capacity for cruelty and evil is only beginning to be displayed with the dismissal of his own mother. One critic of Weiss's novels has remarked of the principal characters, "one would not like to be their friends", and that is as true of the boy, Boëtius von Orlamünde, as it is of the others.

Martin Chalmers